Calculated Risk

A HENRY HOLT MYSTERY

Calculated Risk

Collin Wilcox

Henry Holt and Company
New York

Henry Holt and Company, Inc.
Publishers since 1866
115 West 18th Street
New York, New York 10011

Henry Holt® is a registered
trademark of Henry Holt and Company, Inc.

Library of Congress Cataloging-in-Publication Data
Wilcox, Collin.
Calculated risk / Collin Wilcox.—1st ed.
p.   cm.—(A Henry Holt mystery)
1. Hastings, Frank (Fictitious character)—Fiction.
2. Police— California—San Francisco—Fiction.   I. Title.
PS3573.I395C35   1995   95-9706
813'.54—dc20   CIP
ISBN 0-8050-3003-4

Henry Holt books are available for special promotions and
premiums. For details contact: Director, Special Markets.

First Edition—1995

Designed by Betty Lew

Printed in the United States of America
All first editions are printed on acid-free paper. ∞

10   9   8   7   6   5   4   3   2   1

*This book is dedicated
to Conor, he of
the knowing eyes.*

Calculated
Risk

A HENRY HOLT MYSTERY

1

It was impossible, Hardaway realized, to endure this mewling mumble of self-pity, this endless dirge, this constant paean of despair. It was impossible to look into this face that had once been so responsive, the touch of the poet, the perfection of a Grecian youth, stroking the strings of his lute. Adonis, the essence of erotic grace. All of it corroded by terror, distilled into the bitter brew of the doomed, the lamentations of the dying.

Hardaway glanced at his watch, then stretched his arms overhead, arching his back. The time was almost nine. At Toby's, there was laughter, music—promises to make, promises to keep, the never-ending game.

"So. What d'you think? Toby's?" It was essential, of course, that he extend the invitation. This, too, was part of the game.

Carpenter shook his head. "Not for me." He raised the TV wand. "How about *The Little Foxes*?"

"*The Little Foxes*? Really? What channel?"

"The Movie Channel. Forty-six."

He pretended to consider, let the moment linger between them, all part of the ritual. Then: "I don't think so. Bette Davis—I'm not up for those lips of hers."

"There's no commercials, on forty-six." It was Randy's way of begging. The prospect of being left alone tonight was more than Randy could bear. Tonight, and every night. Call it the HIV blues, some won, others lost. Tonight, drinks at Toby's was the prize.

"I won't be long—an hour or two, no more. Bring you anything?" Hardaway rose, crossed the living room, went to the hall closet. He moved gracefully, easily, aware of his own fluidity. Between them, it was a given that he was the dominant one, the desirable one. Randy was the dreamer, the passive one.

Hardaway pulled on a rough wool lumberjack's shirt that complemented the jeans and Reeboks he'd changed into before dinner. He glanced at Randy, sunk in his armchair, his chin on his chest, still clutching the TV wand. Pouting. For a long, definitive moment the tableau held: one of them with the TV wand, staring at the TV with hollow, hopeless eyes—the other one seeking liberation from the pall that had descended on them; one of them contemplating death, one of them craving life.

" 'An hour or two,' " Carpenter mimicked. He spoke softly, bitterly. "Saturday, it was almost five hours."

"Jesus, Randy, how many times do I have to hear it, about Saturday? You were invited. Brian wanted you to come."

"Brian wanted *you* to come. He thought you'd be more likely to come if he invited me too."

"Randy, I'm not going to respond to that. We've talked this thing to death, about Brian's party. And I'm not going to—"

"Brian's been coming on to you for a year." As Carpenter stared with hot, hollow eyes at the blank TV screen, his voice registered both resignation and accusation.

Still standing in the short hallway that offered escape, a way out, Hardaway struck a helpless pose, arms spread, palms forward, in a plea for reason, for amity. He said nothing. If the other man insisted—cravenly insisted—then he would return to the living room, sit on the sofa, endure *The Little Foxes* while he sipped chardonnay. If, in fact, there was any chardonnay on ice, a doubtful prospect.

Carpenter drew a long, deep breath, his own appeal for reason. Saying: "You get home from work and you change clothes and you go jogging. You get back, and you shower. We make dinner. By eight, eight thirty, we've finished dinner. And now it's nine o'clock, and you're going to Toby's. You're going to—"

"Jesus, Randy, I *asked* you to go. I *invited* you. There's no reason you *shouldn't* go. You're—Christ—you're giving up. Okay, you're sick. Just like half the people we know, you're sick. But did it ever occur to you that—"

"What occurred to me is that you can't bear to be with me for more than an hour a day. You might not even realize it, I'll give you that. But the truth is, you wish you were rid of me."

"Randy . . ." He let the word linger between them, both a threat and a plea. "Randy, that's not true. It's simply not true."

Wearily, Carpenter nodded. Then, as if it possessed great weight, he raised the TV wand, aimed it at the TV. For now— tonight—the confrontation had ended. Moving with self-conscious precision, Hardaway went to the hallway door, turned the knob. Never would Toby's seem so necessary.

2

With an air of gentle resignation, Hardaway placed the empty wineglass on the mahogany bar. The clock behind the bar was set into the center of a garish Klondike movie poster featuring a wild-eyed buxom blonde, bodice gaping over straining breasts, fleeing from a slavering grizzly. The time was exactly eleven o'clock. *The Little Foxes* was doubtless rolling the credits. His bondage beckoned.

He dropped money on the bar, touched hands with the bartender, and slid off the bar stool. On a warm, inviting Tuesday night in May, Toby's was crowded shoulder to shoulder, flank to flank. The beat of the music, the answering urgency of the voices, the raw, rhythmic movements of arousal, all of it throbbed with tribal urgency. Responding, the voices were louder, the laughter more frenetic. A dozen faces smiled meaningfully as Hardaway made his way through the crowd toward the door. Some of the faces were friends', some were strangers'. Voices rose, but the words were lost in the din. Handshakes lingered, accompanied by the smiles, the invitations. From behind, fingers lightly stroked his buttocks.

The sidewalk, too, was crowded. Voices here were pitched to the same register as the voices still audible from inside Toby's. Tonight, the Castro was ready for anything.

At Eighteenth Street he turned right, uphill. Almost immediately, the press of pedestrians eased. Another block, on Collingwood, and the tempo would slacken to what passed for normal in San Francisco. Castro was avaricious, blatantly commercial. Collingwood was restrained, residential. In its few short blocks, Collingwood featured some of the city's most dignified Victorian architecture, mostly three-story town houses, now divided into apartments. The sidewalk trees were decades old.

He turned left, began climbing the first steep block of Collingwood. Their apartment was in the second block, up another hill, this one steeper than the first. Earlier in the evening, jogging, he'd taken these two blocks in good time. Now, after a heavy dinner and three—four—glasses of wine, he would walk. He would—

"Charles."

Instinctively responding, startled, he turned to face the figure materializing from the shadows behind a head-high hedge.

A friend?

No, not a friend.

Hardaway stood motionless, watching as the stranger advanced: a slim black man moving slowly, purposefully. The stranger wore a leather bomber jacket and tight blue jeans, reg-

5

ulation in the Castro. Even the dark glasses conformed to the with-it image the stranger projected. The dark stocking cap, though, was an aberration.

The night was dark, and the sidewalks here were almost deserted. And the Castro could be dangerous, after dark.

And the woman on the phone had threatened him. "You'll die," she'd promised.

He began backing away, moving up the hill. One step. Two steps. Cautiously. Watchfully.

"Hey, Charles, what d'you say?" Still purposefully advancing, the stranger spoke in a soft, lilting ghetto patois, wheedling.

"Who—who are you?"

"Who d'you think I am, Charles? Don't you remember?" Still wheedling. Or were the words really mocking him?

They were almost within reach of each other. Glancing quickly to his right, across the quiet street, Hardaway saw a man and a woman climbing the hill. The woman was laughing at something the man had said.

Quickly, Hardaway turned back to face the black man.

Just as, moving suddenly, silently, a graceful, savage predator, the stranger sprang forward. The pipe struck Hardaway squarely in the solar plexus, a numbing blow. And another blow—and another. He must call out. He must run. But as he wrenched away, stumbling over the curb, he realized that his legs were no longer supporting him. He tried to scream, but heard nothing. He could only raise his right hand against the final blow, to his temple. As he fell, he discovered that he was looking up into the night sky. The ocean fog had come in through the Golden Gate; there were no stars tonight.

His mother—had she heard his scream? Would she—?

3

Hastings raised himself on one elbow, looked across Ann to the nightstand alarm clock. Almost midnight. They'd gone to bed about ten o'clock, both of them with books to read. More than a month ago, they'd taken a vow: no more watching TV in bed, even the late-night news.

By eleven, Ann had yawned, kissed him dutifully, yawned again, and switched off her light. He'd promised not to be long, and by eleven thirty the bedroom had been dark. Beside him, Ann was deep in sleep, softly snoring. Sometimes she asked him whether she snored, whether she kept to her side of the bed, whether she was a restless sleeper. Some women sought the reassurance of "Yes, I love you." Ann asked only about that which she couldn't control, her sleeping self. They'd never talked about love, never said the words. It was, he realized, the nature of their relationship. They'd both been married before, both had children, both suffered when their marriages ended. His ex-wife, a socialite who'd flaunted her affair with a tennis pro, had asked for a divorce. Ann's ex-husband, a psychiatrist who specialized in the neuroses of affluent divorcées, had ended their marriage.

Hastings had met her two years ago, when Ann's teenage son had been a witness to murder, and briefly a suspect. Hastings had contrived to return to Ann's spacious, gracefully furnished Victorian flat often enough to screw up the courage it took to ask her out for dinner at a neighborhood restaurant. Dinner became a weekly event for them, and soon they were lovers. Comfortable, companionable lovers. If Ann's ex-husband took the two sons for the weekend, Hastings spent Saturday night and Sunday morning at Ann's place. Often, though, Ann came to his bachelor apartment in the Marina, with a view across San Francisco Bay to the hills of Marin County. Sometimes they cooked shish kebab in the fireplace and ate it with French bread and a tossed green salad. Sometimes they had crab, bought live at Fisherman's Wharf.

Then, only a few months after they met, during the apprehension of a wild-eyed drug cultist, he'd made the mistake of turning his back on one of the cultist's spaced-out followers. The youth had taken an ancient Mayan war club from a wall display, and put Hastings in the hospital for five days with a concussion. For at least two weeks, the doctors had warned, he should stay in bed convalescing. Ann had picked him up at the hospital. She'd taken him home, moved him into her bedroom. Her two teenage sons had apparently approved. They'd—

Close beside him, muted, the telephone warbled.

"Yes?" Softly.

"It's Canelli, Lieutenant."

"I'll call you right back." He cradled the phone, slipped out of bed, stood for a moment looking down at Ann. She stirred, mumbled something, sighed, went back to sleep. Hastings took his robe from "his" chair, found his slippers under the bed. Moments later, in the living room, he touch-toned the number for the inspector's squadroom. Canelli answered on the third ring as Hastings clicked his ballpoint pen over the notepad that was always kept beside the telephone. During the year he'd lived with Ann and the boys, his only demand had been that there always be a notepad beside the living room phone.

"So?"

"Well," Canelli said, "it's a guy on Collingwood, just up from Eighteenth. Collingwood's just a couple of blocks long, very steep, all residential. The guy was walking up Collingwood from Eighteenth, and another guy stepped out from behind a hedge. Something was said, but it wasn't an argument, no voices raised, nothing like that. But the next thing, the victim was on the ground. There're just two witnesses, a couple who was also walking up Collingwood on the other side of the street from the victim, and a little farther up the hill. They didn't know anything was wrong until the guy was already down, and the assailant was walking down Collingwood to Eighteenth, real calm, it sounds like."

"When'd it happen?"

"About ten minutes after eleven. Call it fifty minutes ago."

"Is the scene secure?"

"No problem. Three cars, five men. Or, really, four men and one woman. Sergeant Serrano, from Mission station, he's in charge. Good man."

"What about the witnesses?"

"Well, they'd been to dinner, on Castro, and they were just

going to get their car and go home. They live out in the Sunset. Serrano talked them into hanging around until one of our guys got there, to talk to them."

"Who's on the board?"

"Well, that's why I'm calling, Lieutenant. I mean, there's that Harris surveillance, which is taking at least six guys, including two of ours. Plus that gang thing out at Hunter's Point, that's still active. So the only one available from our squad is"—a momentary pause—"is Janet Collier."

In the other man's voice, Hastings could clearly hear it: the subtle reticence, the suggestion of discomfort. It was the price he knew he'd pay for arranging Janet Collier's transfer to Homicide. Intuition was a good detective's principal tool.

Meaning that every man in his command certainly sensed that Hastings had fallen in love with Janet Collier.

He hadn't meant for it to happen. He'd been shorthanded on a stakeout, and Janet had been available—

"Lieutenant?"

"Sorry." He cleared his throat. Saying: "Send Collier. Tell her she'll be the officer of record. I'll meet her at the scene."

"Yessir."

4

"Joseph Serrano," the squat, chunky sergeant said, introducing himself.

"Frank Hastings." He nodded, smiled, offered his hand. Then, in unison, the two ranking officers at the scene turned to face the figure sprawled on the sidewalk. In the dim light from the tree-lined block's two streetlamps, the figure was amorphous, no more than a lump of lifeless flesh covered by clothing. With its blood no longer circulating, the lump was flattened at the bottom. Because the muscles had gone slack, excrement combined with the rivulet of blood that had run down the gutter. The figure lay on its back, head and shoulders in the gutter, torso and legs on the sidewalk.

"I've called the crime lab and the coroner," Hastings said.

As he spoke, he saw Janet Collier. Standing about fifteen feet uphill from the body, she was talking to a middle-aged woman who wore a coat over her nightgown. She was gesticulating, pointing up the hill to the next block.

"No one's touched the body," Hastings said. It was a statement, not a question.

"I don't see how," Serrano answered promptly. "We know when he was killed, from the primary witnesses. They had him eyeballed from the time he went down to when the first unit arrived. He was killed at ten minutes after eleven, maybe fifteen minutes after, but no more. Someone phoned nine-one-one, and we had a car on the scene three minutes after the call went out. And there he was." Serrano gestured to the body.

"So no one could've touched him without being observed either by you or by witnesses. Is that what you're saying?"

"Yessir, that's what I'm saying."

Hastings nodded, thanked the other man, and stepped over the yellow tapes, at the same time gesturing for Janet to join him. He watched her break off her conversation with the middle-aged woman. Nodding her thanks as she turned away, Janet Collier ducked under the tapes, joined Hastings as he waited a few feet from the body. They stood side by side, both of them staring down at the body.

Aware that the uniformed officers were watching, Hastings held himself stiffly, correctly. His voice matched his manner: precise, aloof. "So what d'you think?"

Also holding herself correctly, slightly removed, she pointed down the hill. "He was apparently walking up from Eighteenth Street, alone. The assailant was probably hiding behind that hedge." She pointed again. "There were only two witnesses. They were on the other side of the street, also walking up the hill. They were a little ahead of the victim, so they didn't actually see the blow struck. They heard the victim cry out, though, and they turned quickly enough to see him fall. By that time, the assailant was escaping—walking down Collingwood to Eighteenth. They say he turned right, toward Castro. He wasn't running, they said. He was walking. Very calmly."

Hastings gestured for Janet to stand aside while he held his breath against the stench of excrement and knelt beside the body. In the gutter, the head lay in a pool of blood that ran downhill from the body. Except for the bloody head, there was no other indication of trauma. The arms were flung wide, the legs were crooked. The victim's eyes were open, rolled up in his head.

Hastings rose, exhaled, stepped back. "These witnesses— are they cooperative? Reliable?"

Collier nodded decisively. "Absolutely reliable, I'd say. They're in their late twenties, very bright, very conscientious, very well spoken—yuppies, I guess. College grads, no question."

"You've got their addresses, phone numbers?"

"Of course." The reply came stiffly.

Ignoring her muted indignation, he said, "How'd they describe the assailant?"

"Tall and slim, moved like a young man, they thought. Dressed casually. They thought he might be black, but that's just a guess, I think. He was probably wearing a stocking cap. But the light here—just two streetlights for the whole block . . ." She gestured, shrugged.

"So what else? Anything?"

"That lady I was talking to . . ." She pointed to the overweight gray-haired woman wearing a coat over her nightgown, then pointed to a nearby small one-story Victorian house, authentically restored. "She came out of her house about eleven thirty, after the area was secure. She recognized the victim. Not by name, but by looks. She says he lived in the next block, about halfway up the hill. She says—"

"Lieutenant." It was Serrano, hesitantly interrupting. The sergeant was standing beside a man of medium height, medium weight, medium age. Meticulously barbered and groomed, he was wearing the after-dark clothing indigenous to the culture of the Castro: tight blue jeans, a working man's jacket, running shoes. A subtle mix of mannerisms suggested that the man standing beside Serrano was gay. The man was badly shaken, repeatedly swallowing, licking his lips, then swallowing again. His complexion was pallid. His eyes were hunted; he couldn't quite stand still.

Hastings moved expectantly toward Serrano, who spoke guardedly across the yellow tape: "This is Graham Blair, Lieutenant. He knows the victim."

Hastings stepped back over the tape, drew Serrano and Graham Blair to the rear of a parked police cruiser. Hastings took out his notebook and flipped to a clear page, ready to copy down Blair's address and phone numbers. Blair lived on Russian Hill, across the city. Having taken down the information, Hastings turned to a fresh notebook page. Saying: "And the victim? What's his name?"

"It's Charles."

Hastings wrote "Charles," then looked expectantly at the other man. "Last name?"

"Sorry." Blair's uncertain smile was apologetic. "I don't know his last name. I just see him once in a while."

As the witness was speaking, Hastings had motioned for

Janet to join them. "Where'd you see him?" she asked. "How often?"

"Well . . ." Blair shrugged, frowned, licked his lips, blinked, swallowed spasmodically. "Well, maybe once a month, I'd say, something like that. Mostly at Toby's."

"Toby's?" Hastings asked.

But Janet had the answer: "The bar," she said, addressing Blair. "On Castro."

Visibly reassured, plainly yearning to make contact with someone sympathetic, Blair nodded. "Right. Just off Eighteenth."

"Were you at Toby's tonight?" Hastings asked.

"Yes, I was."

"And was Charles there, too?"

Blair nodded. "Yes, he was."

"Did you speak to him?"

"No, I didn't. I'd gone to a movie, and I just stopped by Toby's for a drink. I saw Charles in the crowd, that's all."

"But you've talked to him in the past. You know him."

Blair considered carefully. "I've said a few things to him. But we weren't friends, or even acquaintances. I just knew him by sight, that's all."

"Considering that you didn't really know the victim," Collier said, "you're pretty upset. Why's that, Mr. Blair?"

As if he were trying to assess the real significance of the question, he studied her face for a moment. Then he spoke hesitantly, but with obvious determination: "I'm a gay man, Miss—?"

"Collier. Inspector Janet Collier."

Staring down at the body, his manner projecting the most abject despair, Blair spoke heavily: "It's hard, you know. Being gay, I mean. Even in San Francisco—even in the Castro—it's hard."

Hastings exchanged a glance with Janet, who shrugged. She had no more questions. Hastings spoke to the witness. "I guess that'll do it for now, Mr. Blair. You aren't planning to leave town, are you?"

"N—no. Not really."

"We'll be talking to you, then. And thanks for coming forward." Hastings gestured to Collier, and they recrossed the yellow tapes together. At the corner of Eighteenth, he saw the white coroner's van making the turn into Collingwood. Hastings stepped to the body, used one rubber-clad forefinger to expose the front pockets of the rough woolen lumberjack shirt the victim was wearing, shirttail out. As he'd hoped, he found a wallet. Gingerly, he extracted the wallet as Collier produced a small high-intensity flashlight. An examination of the victim's driver's license yielded everything they needed: First name, Charles. Last name, Hardaway. Age, thirty-five. Residence, 234 Collingwood.

Hastings checked the wallet, which contained twenty-three dollars. He handed the wallet to Collier, who was ready with a clear plastic evidence bag and a ballpoint pen to identify the evidence.

"I'll go ring his bell," Hastings said, "see what happens. You stay here, make sure everything gets done right. Wait for me. I'll sign the releases. If anything comes up"—from an inside pocket he produced a miniature surveillance radio—"we'll use channel three." As he spoke, he switched on the radio, clicked the channel selector to 3.

Collier was doing the same. The radio check was normal. "Any questions?" he asked.

"No questions."

"Remember," Hastings said, "be picky. Picky is what Homicide is all about. Take your time, do it right. Never forget about the chain of evidence. That's all the DAs care about, a good chain of evidence." He ventured a smile.

"Picky." Spontaneously, she returned the smile. "Gotcha."

5

The images tumbled and tossed and whirled in the darkness of the void: himself as a child. His mother, holding him close. His father, glowering. Fritz, his dog, whining and barking. All of it smothering him, then leaving him alone, crying. And the clangor—the sharp, piercing mechanical warble:

The door buzzer. Someone was at the door.

Eyes open now, he realized that his gaze was fixed on the TV screen. It was an old movie, black and white. Warner Baxter, dressed in top hat and tails.

The buzzer sounded again, more insistently.

Confused, he dropped his gaze to his hand. Yes, he still held the TV wand. In the dimly lit living room he blinked, focused on the wand, then touched the power button.

The time
God, the time
Ten minutes after one o'clock, his watch read. Two hours after Charles had promised to come home. And now, drunk, having lost his key, Charles was at the front door, demanding admittance.

How had Charles lost his keys? His jeans—he'd met someone at Toby's, and they'd gone home, and when he'd slipped off his jeans, the keys had fallen to the floor. Brian—at Toby's, Charles had met Brian, gone home with him. They'd—

Once more, the buzzer sounded, a remorseless peal. Half a minute. A full minute, and more.

He placed the wand on a lamp table, braced both hands on the arms of his easy chair, levered himself laboriously to his feet. How humiliating, that he must wrestle with his own body, the contest that, day by day, week by week, he was losing. As a child, he had run in the park with his dog. All day long, he ran.

He was making his way to the door. He realized that his eyes were stinging. Tears of self-pity were almost blinding him. He turned the knob, let the door come open—and faced a stranger on the landing. A big, trim, heavily muscled man wearing casual khakis, a dark green nylon windbreaker, and loafers. Mid-forties, calm brown eyes, unremarkable features, dark brown hair, a quiet voice, somehow compelling:

"Is this Charles Hardaway's residence?" As he spoke, the stranger produced a leather folder, open in his palm.

A gold badge . . .

Police.

At ten minutes after one o'clock, the police had come.

The policeman was waiting for a reply, patiently—but watchfully, implacably.

"Charles," he faltered. "It's Charles." Suddenly he slumped against the entryway wall, for support.

"Did he live here?"

"Oh, God, you say *'did'*? Is that what you said? You're saying that—" His throat closed. Palpably, he could feel his strength draining away, leaving him helpless, still slumped against the wall, head lowered. It was, he knew, shock. He'd once done volunteer work for the Red Cross. He'd learned to recognize shock in others. Now, in the wee hours, it was his turn.

"May I have your name, sir?"

"Yes. It—it's—" He swallowed. "It's Carpenter. Randall Carpenter. Randy."

"Do you live here, Mr. Carpenter?"

"Y—yes. I—we—" He broke off, began shaking his head. His legs were beginning to tremble.

"Listen," the policeman was saying as he moved a half-step closer. "Let's go inside, sit down."

"But I—"

"Do it," the policeman ordered quietly. "Sit down. I'll get you a glass of water. Then we'll talk. Here . . ." He grasped Carpenter's forearm in a firm grip, turned him, led him to a sofa, waited until he was seated. Then the policeman returned to the front door, locked it, and asked for directions to the kitchen, and the glasses.

As he gulped down half a glass of water, Carpenter watched the detective over the rim of the glass. When Carpenter set the glass aside, the policeman said, "My name is Frank Hastings. I'm a lieutenant in Homicide, co-commander of the squad. And you're right. I've come about Charles Hardaway." He spoke in a quiet, neutral voice. His gaze remained locked on Carpenter's face, making remorseless eye contact. "Did you see Hardaway today?"

"I—I." Carpenter frowned, an expression of desperate bafflement. "I don't know what you mean."

"I mean," Hastings said, "that I'd like to know the last time you saw him. When, and where."

"It—it was here. It was about nine o'clock. Charles decided to—to get out. Just for an hour or two, no more. He—" Once more, his throat closed. Then, in a low, coarse whisper, begging, he said, "Tell me what happened. You've got to tell me what happened. Please."

Hastings drew a deep, regretful breath, then spoke softly, gravely: "Charles apparently went to Toby's for a few drinks. He apparently left Toby's a little after eleven. He walked to Eighteenth Street, walked to Collingwood, and turned up the hill. He was probably coming here—coming home. He'd only come a block on Collingwood when someone attacked him. It was probably a beating, we don't know the cause of death yet. But he—"

Carpenter spoke without conscious thought, reacting to some blind, urgent imperative: "Eleven o'clock, you say. He left Toby's at eleven?"

Hastings nodded. "About eleven. Yes."

"Alone, you say. He left Toby's alone." He spoke insistently, demanding the most precise accuracy. Because it was all that mattered, now. It was all that would remain. Charles hadn't gone with Brian. He'd been coming home. Just as he'd promised, he was coming home.

"And he's dead." It was a statement, all hope surrendered. He could see the truth plain in the detective's eyes, downcast and regretful. They'd killed Charles. Gay-bashing in the Castro, bully boys. Skinheads, getting their rocks off.

"Yes," Hastings answered. "Yes, he's dead. He died quickly, I think. I think he fell and hit his head on the curb." The detective cleared his throat. Adding tentatively: "If that helps."

Carpenter drained the glass of water. Then he drew up his feet close to the sofa, levered himself to stand erect. "I'm going to make a drink. Bourbon. Do you want one?"

"No, thanks. I don't drink."

Carpenter nodded, went slowly into the kitchen, opened the overhead cupboard where they kept the liquor. He poured bourbon into a short glass, closed the cupboard door. Walking carefully, he returned to the living room, lowered himself into an armchair. Holding the glass in both hands, he gulped. Once, twice. After he placed the glass on the table, he said, "The reason I get around so slowly, it's because I have AIDS."

"Ah . . ." Hastings nodded. "Yes. I see." He let a moment pass. "You and Charles Hardaway, you're—roommates."

Carpenter smiled, an exhausted, defeated admission of utter despair. "You can say it, Lieutenant."

"I—"

As if he were instructing a reluctant pupil, Carpenter spoke with exaggerated patience: "The word is *lovers*. We were lovers, Charles and I. For years, we've been lovers."

"And you—you depended on him."

"Yes. I depended on him."

Hastings nodded. It was an effort to convey a policeman's sympathy for this sad, frail, dying man. But it was a sympathy Hastings knew he would never feel. Looking for votes, the mayor had once decreed that a psychologist be hired to instruct the members of the Inspectors' Bureau in gay awareness. Hastings had managed to miss all but one session.

With a businesslike gesture, he took out his notebook, found a fresh page. "What I'd like," he said, "is for you to tell me everything you can about Charles Hardaway. Start with the statistics—age, occupation, previous residence, things like that."

"My God." Carpenter gulped more bourbon. "Can't it wait? This whole thing, I—I can't handle it. I—"

"If you want us to find out who killed him, get the guy locked up, you're going to have to cooperate, Mr. Carpenter. Now. Right now. In homicides like this the more time that elapses, the worse our chance of closing the case."

"I know. But, Jesus, I—"

"How old was Hardaway?"

"Thirty-five, last month." It was no more than a whisper.

"Occupation?"

"Draftsman."

"Do you know the name of his employer?"

"Stansfield and Baker. They're in San Mateo."

"Do you know how long he worked for Stansfield and Baker?"

"About two years. Before that, he worked for Buchnel."

"You said you and Charles were together for years. How many years, exactly?"

"Almost three years."

"And before that, what do you know about Charles Hardaway?"

Carpenter shrugged. "It's a pretty common story. He grew up in Detroit, and did the usual things—went to Michigan State, but dropped out after a couple of years. Went back to Detroit, got a drafting job, married a girl he'd known since the first grade. She had a baby—a boy. All that lasted until Charles turned thirty, when he came out. He apologized to his wife, who knew it was coming—and to his mother, who cried—and to his father, who broke his nose. He came to San Francisco and had his nose fixed. He got the job at Buchnel, and found a nice apartment, just a few blocks from here. Then, of course, Buchnel found out he was gay, and they fired him. He didn't care. He'd saved some money, and he spent a couple of months in Europe. I met him just after he'd come back. I had this apartment, and I was looking for someone. I'd just gotten out of a relationship, and . . ." Carpenter's voice trailed off, his eyes lost focus, blurred by pain. In his narrow, wasted face, the lines of despair were deeply etched.

"And so Hardaway moved in here."

Carpenter nodded.

"About three years ago."

"Yes."

"Did Hardaway have any enemies, anyone who'd threatened him, carried a grudge against him?"

As if the question caused physical discomfort, Carpenter winced, then shook his head. "N—no. Everyone liked Charles. *Everyone.* He was so wonderful, so carefree. And so—" Once more, Carpenter faltered before finally saying in a whisper, "So beautiful. So very beautiful."

Momentarily Hastings's thoughts shifted to the amorphous body sprawled half in the gutter, only a block away. What should he do, if Carpenter wanted to see his lover's body? What would he say?

"But someone wanted him dead," Hastings said. "Someone hated him enough to kill him."

"Somebody got drunk, and decided to do a little gay-bashing," Carpenter retorted bitterly. "Every weekend in the Castro, it happens. The only difference, this time, it went too far. Usually it's a broken nose, or a ruptured spleen. Or maybe someone loses an eye, or they get a leg broken. That's the current fad: find a fag, punch him out, then put his leg across a curb, and jump on it. But those stories never get in the papers or on TV."

"I know about gay-bashing." Hastings spoke quietly, in an

attempt to focus the other man's attention on his words. "And this doesn't fit the pattern. Gay-bashers travel in packs. Or, at least, two or three. They're usually drunk, and they're loud. None of that fits the information we have on this case. We're talking about one man who did a very good, quiet job of attacking Charles Hardaway."

Dropping his gaze, sitting slumped, head hanging, dejection personified, Carpenter made no response.

"Tomorrow," Hastings said, "I'll be sending someone to get the victim's effects. Not his personal effects. Not clothing, or jewelry. We'll want correspondence and records—things that show his financial situation, and his associations, his past life. Also—" Hastings broke off. Now came the hard part: "Also, tomorrow, we'll need to have the, ah, victim identified."

Without moving, or raising his head, Carpenter mumbled, "I knew that was coming."

"If there's anyone else—a relative . . ." Hastings let it go unfinished.

Numbly, Carpenter shook his head. "He's got a sister. Helen. She lives in LA. But—" As if to order his thoughts, Carpenter broke off. Finally, with great effort, he raised his eyes to engage Hastings. "But I—I guess I'll do it. I mean, somebody's got to. So it should be me."

"I'll send someone in the morning. She'll be examining Mr. Hardaway's effects—his papers, as I said. Her name is Collier. Inspector Janet Collier. She'll take you to the—ah—morgue."

"And then, afterwards, they do the autopsy."

"It's the law. If someone dies without a doctor signing a death certificate, then the law says that—"

"I know all that." For the first time, Carpenter spoke sharply, a quick flare of temper. "I know all that," he repeated. "I live in the Castro, don't forget. So I know about that."

6

For almost a half hour, talking steadily, in great detail, Hastings had been recapping the Carpenter interrogation. During that whole time Collier had hardly interrupted him. They were standing together outside the circle of bright white light cast by battery-powered floodlamps that were focused on the body. Floyd Gregg, one of three assistant MEs, was consulting his clipboard with an air of finality. Speaking to Hastings, Janet Collier said, "I think the techs are almost finished."

Hastings moved closer to the yellow tape, for a final look at Charles Hardaway's face. Even in death, it was handsome. The blood-soaked hair was dark blond, worn earlobe-long. Improbably, the hair was hardly mussed. The eyes, half open, were brown. The features were pleasingly proportioned. In life, with his slim, trim body and his beautifully styled hair and his narcissist's good looks, Charles Hardaway would have attracted second looks from either sex.

Returning to Janet Collier, Hastings asked, "Any more witnesses?"

She shook her head. "Not so far. No weapon, either. Nothing."

While he watched two police lab technicians at work, one of them taking pictures, one of them searching methodically for evidence in the quadrants he'd chalked off on the sidewalk and the gutter where the body lay, Hastings continued to summarize his interview with Randall Carpenter. As he talked, Hastings was physically aware of Janet Collier's presence as she stood beside him. She wore a leather bomber jacket, slacks, and lugged high-top hiking boots. In the last two hours, the fog from the ocean had crept through the valleys of the city closest to the water, and a chill had settled on the Castro district, where two valleys converged. Against the fog, Collier had zipped her jacket up to her chin; her hands were tucked into the jacket's slash pockets. She wore her dark brown hair in a ponytail, her standard on-duty solution to the hair problem. She was a small woman with an oval face, quick hazel eyes, and a small, determined chin. Her manner was straightforward. In the squadroom, she seldom smiled at casual banter, never engaged in sexual innuendo. Neither did she frequent the two cop bars near the Hall of Justice. The single mother of a teenage boy, Janet Collier spent most evenings either helping her son with his homework or reading departmental training manuals.

When Hastings had finished describing the Carpenter interrogation, Collier shook her head sympathetically. "Poor guy. It sounds like he's scared to death. He's got AIDS, and he's afraid he'll die alone. God, it must be terrible."

Still staring at the men working over the body, Hastings decided to say, "He should've been more careful. It's not like he has pneumonia, or cancer—things he can't help. AIDS is behavior-based."

"Except that the incubation time can be ten years, at least. A lot of the guys who're dying now never heard of AIDS when they contracted it."

"I don't think your arithmetic is right." He spoke in a flat, uncompromising voice.

For a moment she made no reply. Then, speaking with the quiet, purposeful stubbornness that Hastings was learning to predict, she said, "You blame them."

He realized that, either now or later, this was a matter that must be settled between them. Drawing a deep, reluctant breath, he said, "If they're acquainted with the risk—death—and they still choose to indulge in high-risk sexual behavior, then they're taking their chances."

"You're prejudiced against gays." She said it softly; the words were shaded by something that might be regret.

"I suppose that, if I'm honest, then—yes—I'm prejudiced against men who have sex with other men. It . . ." He spread his hands as he searched for the words. "It's unnatural."

"Lieutenant." It was Floyd Gregg, who was standing beside the body.

Hastings turned to face Janet directly as he said, "Time out?" He made the T sign with his hands. She was answering his conciliatory smile, nodding.

"Time out."

"Right back." He stepped over the tape.

"I'm finished. Want us to move him, wrap it up?" As he spoke, Gregg stifled a yawn, glanced at his watch.

"What about the weapon? What was it?"

Gregg used a rubber-gloved hand to draw back the victim's woolen shirt, which had been unbuttoned, and lifted up the white T-shirt. On the pale flesh of the torso Hastings saw two welts, both about six inches long. The welts were parallel, one across the stomach, one across the chest.

"Looks like a club," Gregg said. "Maybe an iron pipe, something like that. We'll know more when we get him on the table."

"What about the head wound? That's what killed him, probably."

"I agree. But, again, we got to get him on the table, tomorrow, if you want something definite."

"Anything else?"

"No, sir." Gregg handed over a clipboard with a coroner's on-site release form attached. Hastings scanned the document, signed, dated, and timed it, and returned it to Gregg, with thanks. He stepped back over the yellow tape to stand beside Janet Collier. As he did, he realized that he should have allowed her to examine the body before it was signed off. He glanced at her face, but saw nothing that suggested displeasure. Instead, she spoke matter-of-factly:

"Anything significant?"

"It looks like—" Hastings glanced over his shoulder, broke off as a lab technician came close, then moved away. According to protocol, the information discussed by inspectors on the scene of a homicide was privileged. "It looks like a club, maybe a pipe, or a blackjack. We'll know more tomorrow."

"One of the witnesses—the young woman walking up the hill—she said she saw the assailant swing his arm wide, like a roundhouse punch."

"What else did she say?"

"She said it was very quick. And very quiet, too. I already told you that."

"I get the feeling that this was planned, maybe by someone who saw Hardaway in Toby's. I don't think it was a random gay-bashing. That's not the feeling I'm getting."

"I agree," Collier said. "Except that I don't think the victim was followed from Toby's. I think the assailant was waiting for him. Hiding."

"Meaning," Hastings mused, "that the assailant knew where Hardaway was going—and when."

For a moment neither of them spoke as they watched Gregg and two others straighten the body, put it on a gurney, cover it with a green tarpaulin, and strap it down. As the body was loaded into the coroner's van, Janet said, "What about Hardaway's lover? Randall Carpenter? Did he know Hardaway was going to Toby's?"

"I think so," Hastings answered.

"Maybe they had a lovers' quarrel. Maybe they were breaking up. Maybe Hardaway had just told Carpenter that he was leaving him. Maybe Carpenter couldn't handle it. He's got AIDS. Who else would take care of him, if Hardaway leaves? The more Carpenter thinks about it, the more furious he gets. He knows Hardaway's going to Toby's, and he knows what route he'll take, coming back. So he gets a baseball bat, or a pipe, whatever, and he goes down the block. And he waits. He conceals the club in the shrubbery." She gestured to a thick hedge nearby. "When Hardaway appears, they talk for a minute. Then, when they're standing just a couple of feet from each other, out comes the club. It—"

"Hey." Smiling, moving a whimsical step closer, he raised his hand, a traffic cop's command to stop. "Hey, slow down. You've got Carpenter convicted before you even lay eyes on him." Widening the smile, a suggestion of intimacy, he moved another step closer.

Instantly—reflexively—she backed away. Meaning that he, too, must back off, neutral corners. To signify that he understood, he spoke now in clipped officialese, the lieutenant addressing a subordinate:

"Everything's done here, practically, and it's two o'clock in the morning. Carpenter isn't going anywhere tonight, I'll guarantee that. So I'll go home. The lab guys shouldn't be too much longer. You sign them off, then you go home, too. Tomorrow morning, I want you to pick up Carpenter and take him to the morgue, for the identification. He'll be at his most vulnerable, so keep your eyes open. Plan on picking him up about nine o'clock. By ten o'clock, you should be back at Carpenter's apartment. I've asked him to give us access to Hardaway's papers. Get them, and bring them down to the Hall. Get them copied; five sets should be enough."

"What about Carpenter? How should I handle him?"

"Get as much information as you can, but keep him calm. For now, we'll handle this as a random killing that might've been a gay-bashing—some skinhead creep doing the Castro."

"But you just said—"

"I said it doesn't *feel* like a gay-bashing. But that's just a hunch. The evidence points the other way."

"But we don't *have* any evidence. No weapon, no discarded clothing, nothing. All we have're the witnesses' statements, plus Carpenter's statements. We don't—"

"Jesus, Janet, the guy's only been dead for three hours. Let's take it one step at a time. Tomorrow, you'll help Carpenter make the identification. In the process, you get whatever information you can on the victim, the more you get the better. You also get Carpenter's life story. Then let's meet at the Hall at two o'clock, see what we've got. Okay?"

"Yes, sir."

They stood facing each other for a long, tentative moment as Hastings considered what next to say—and what not to say. Was the wee hour on a fog-swept hill in a quiet residential neighborhood the time for a commander's lecture on proper police procedure?

Was this the time for another man-to-woman overture, one more try?

As the technicians began dismantling their equipment, Hastings made his decision: "This is your first homicide, Janet—the first one you've been in on from the beginning. Everyone, that first time, does exactly what you're doing. They spend a lot of time theorizing. That's understandable. From my point of view it's desirable. I happen to enjoy sorting through a lot of theories. But that's me. The DAs, on the other hand, only deal in facts. And, bottom line, the DAs call the shots."

"So what're you saying?" In the question Hastings could clearly hear a defensive edge. Janet was slow to take criticism—and sometimes quick to take offense. She was a quick-thinking woman with an incredibly exciting body and a mind all her own. Janet couldn't—wouldn't—be pushed around.

"What I'm saying is let's go slow on this. Let's make damn sure we're on solid ground, with evidence. I don't have to tell you that in San Francisco gays have a lot of political clout. They're smart, and they're organized. They're also hated by a lot of people. Which is why we want to go right down the middle on this. Because if we *aren't* down the middle, the first person I'll hear from, sure as hell, will be our beloved Chief Dwyer. And the first person you'll hear from, sure as hell, will be me." Hastings smiled, touched her forearm in a gesture that could mean anything. "See you tomorrow." He spoke softly. "Two o'clock. Right?"

"Right." She watched him turn away and walk down the hill

to his car. For a big man, he moved with remarkable grace. She was aware of the pleasure she felt watching him. It was all there: the economy of movement that fitted perfectly with his slow, thoughtful speech, his reputation for thinking before he acted. And, yes, his reputation for calm, cool courage.

For months, she'd watched him. Many times, she could have contrived to speak to him, but then she'd faltered. It was the irrational, painfully confused shyness of the teenager. She'd even felt herself blush when she was near him.

And then, four months ago, in the incredible luck of the draw, she'd been assigned at random to help with the apprehension of a murder suspect: a slight, self-effacing waiter named Rivak who'd murdered five men. The confrontation became a stalemate, with Hastings and the suspect alone in the suspect's apartment. The door had been bolted from the inside. The suspect had been holding a semiautomatic pistol on Hastings. She'd been ordered to wait in the hallway outside the suspect's apartment. Just wait. She'd heard the shot. But then, instantly, Hastings had called out: it was all right. Moments later, she and three other officers were inside the apartment. They were surrounding the suspect's body as he sat in an easy chair. Because the bullet had entered the brain and hadn't exited, the suspect's eyes had been bulging. Everywhere, there was blood.

It had been her first dead body, and she'd felt her stomach contract as the periphery of her vision began to darken. Hastings had gestured for her to join him in the bedroom. He'd told her to sit on the bed. He'd used the bedside telephone to call the lab and the coroner. They'd been sitting side by side on the bed. From the living room, she'd heard a detective and two uniformed men making jokes, to ease the tension.

Then she had realized that Hastings was holding her hand. And so it had started between them.

7

Objectively, he realized that his hand was trembling slightly as he took the pay phone from its hook. At midnight, the hotel lobby was somnolent. Several overdressed tourists and a few jaded refugees from the banquet circuit were traversing the lobby, some in the direction of the bar, some making for the elevators. Behind the desk, two young women eyed their guests with obvious indifference. The women were dressed in identical uniforms. Their hair was the same shade of tawny blond, their coiffures were modified Farrah Fawcett styles. One of them was yawning, delicately covering her mouth with a perfectly manicured hand. On the customers' side of the desk, also discreetly yawning, a bellhop was dressed in the same gold-piped beige uniform.

34

Would they remember him?

Could they, therefore, identify him?

At the thought, he shifted in the phone cubicle, turned his back on the registration desk. If he drew a deep breath just before he placed the call, would it steady him? Or, like his trembling hands, would a deep breath turn tremulous and betray him?

It was, he decided, a risk that must be taken. Never must she suspect the depth of his fear.

With an unsteady forefinger, he touch-toned her number. She answered on the second ring:

"Yes?"

But at that same instant he realized that, incredibly, he hadn't rehearsed what he meant to say.

"*Yes?*"

"I—ah—" Suddenly his throat closed. Desperately, he tried again to speak, but failed.

"Is it done?" she asked. "Is that it?"

He realized that he was nodding at the phone. "Y—yes. It's—yes—it's—" Once more, his voice failed. But now it no longer mattered.

Because this was murder.

Murder.

"It—it's done. But there was a—a problem."

"A problem." Her voice was totally uninflected.

"He—he died. It was—"

"Don't call me again on this line. Later today, I'll call you with another number. Understood?"

"Y—yes. Understood."

The line clicked, went dead.

8

"*Dammit!*" Hastings thumped the wristwatch with his middle finger.

Seated across the lunch table, Friedman drank the last of his coffee before he asked, "Battery shot?"

"I guess so." Hastings shook his wrist, looked ruefully at the watch. "What time is it?"

"Twenty to two." Friedman signaled the waitress for their check. "When're you meeting Janet?"

"Two o'clock."

"Want me to sit in? I don't have to be in court till three."

"Fine." Hastings pointed to the waitress approaching with their check. "Odd? Even?"

"Even," Friedman answered promptly. But the number of their check ended in 5. Friedman groaned, produced a credit card. At almost two hundred forty pounds, the unofficial departmental upper limit, Friedman was at least twenty-five pounds overweight. He was an amiable, elliptical, often inscrutable man: cops and criminals, he chose to keep both sides guessing. When Captain Kreiger, commander of Homicide, had died of a heart attack as he was urinating in the department's fourth-floor men's room, Friedman had been offered command of Homicide. First he'd declined. Then he'd countered. He would share the job with Hastings: two lieutenants, co-commanding a squad that averaged a dozen inspectors, currently eleven men and one woman. When Friedman had offered the deal to Hastings, the junior lieutenant had also declined. He knew he couldn't handle the departmental politics that went with the job. "Hell," Friedman had said, "I can't handle them either. But if we don't take the job, sure as hell, they'll move Jeffries over, from Vice. And Jeffries is an asshole, it's an established fact."

Hastings had conceded the point, and accepted the offer. Friedman, they'd agreed, would be the inside man, the tactician. Hastings would work in the field—away from deputy chiefs and other job-related problems.

"So what've we got," Friedman said, "on the Collingwood thing?"

"What we've got is someone who got clubbed to death as he was walking home from a gay bar. Period. No weapon, no apparent motive. No robbery. No fuss, no muss. Thirty seconds, and the assailant was walking away."

As Friedman signed the check and retrieved his credit card, he said, "I hate cases like this. There's nothing there—no place to start, no handle. Odds are, it's a random killing, no motive, except for the kick some creep got when he was committing murder."

"Let's see what Janet found when she talked to Carpenter."

Friedman flicked a glance at Hastings's face, but for the moment said nothing. Hastings knew that mannerism. Friedman was about to render a judgment. Friedman's face was broad and swarthy; his dark eyes were unrevealing. His thick brown hair, generously streaked with gray, was never quite combed. His mouth was habitually pursed. It was a poker player's face—a winner's face, slightly smug.

"How's Janet working out?" Friedman asked. It was a bland question, but Hastings knew where it was leading. He decided on a first strike:

"She's doing great. She's smart, and she works hard. She's a good interrogator, too. She has a feel for it. She knows when to keep quiet and listen."

"She's also got a feeling for keeping the guys in the squadroom in line. With a body like hers, that's a neat trick."

Finishing his own coffee, Hastings made no reply. He knew there was more.

"Some guys," Friedman said, "seem to doubt their masculinity if they aren't hitting on good-looking women. But like I said, Janet handles it just right. I hear, a few years back, when she was in Bunco, she got involved with Kellerman, in Vice. That was before he took the job with the feds. The affair cost her, but she learned from it. Which is where I started with this—complimenting her. She's cultivated the light touch, and most of the guys are happy to go along. She's liked, is what I'm saying. She plays by the rules."

"I'm glad to hear you say it."

"But then . . ." Friedman dropped his voice to a more significant note. They'd come, Hastings knew, to the crux of the matter: "Then," Friedman repeated, "inevitably, there're the assholes. Marsten, for instance."

Hastings began drawing designs on the white tablecloth with the tines of his fork.

"Marsten," Friedman said, "has a plan. As always."

No response.

"Marsten is after your job," Friedman said. "As always. Except that, this time around, he figures he's got an angle."

Hastings concentrated on embellishing the tablecloth design.

"He figures you lust after Janet Collier. Therefore, he figures that if he really comes on to her, makes a big thing of it in the squadroom, then you'll get involved. Which, obviously, would be a big mistake. Which is exactly what Marsten wants you to do—make a big mistake." Friedman paused for emphasis. Then, speaking with quiet precision: "Which is why, of course, office romances are a bad idea."

Still working on the design, eyes lowered, carefully considering his response, Hastings waited until he was sure the other man had finished. Then, raising his eyes, he said, "We talked about this when we hired her, Pete. That's almost three months ago."

"The first year's always provisional."

"Does that mean you want to send her back to Bunco? Is that what you're saying?" Hastings made no effort to hide his sudden flare of anger.

"It means," Friedman said, his voice dead level, "that she's been here for three months. She's due for a review."

"Her work is first-rate."

Friedman nodded solemnly. "No question. None."

"But it's not her work we're talking about."

Deeply reluctant, Friedman drew a long breath. "That's true, Frank. We aren't talking about Janet's work."

"We're talking about me."

Once more, Friedman nodded. For a long moment they stared at each other across the remains of their lunch. Finally Friedman spoke: "We've never discussed it in so many words, but after all these years, I figure we're friends. I figure that we care what happens to each other."

"Of course." It was an exasperated response. But a quick glance at Friedman's face revealed that the other man understood the exasperation, no damage done.

"Which is why," Friedman went on, "I feel compelled to tell you that, from where I sit, it looks to me like you're making a mistake. Which is to say, it looks to me like you and Janet are an item." He let a beat pass, hopeful of a response. When none came, he said, "Now, in ordinary circumstances, we wouldn't even be talking about this. But the point is, these aren't ordinary circumstances. These are problems that could affect the smooth-running operation of what I like to think is one of the best homicide operations in the country."

"What d'you mean by 'item'?" Hastings was satisfied with his dead-level response.

"You know what I mean."

"I guess you know," Hastings answered, "that you're about the only person I'd even be discussing this with."

"I take that as a compliment. So thanks."

For another moment Hastings stared at the other man. Then, in precisely measured phrases, he said, "Janet and I were on the scene in the Rivak suicide, and we were both shook up. She'd never seen a dead one, and I'd never had brains spattered on my shirt. We helped each other through it, and I admired the way she handled herself. During the next few weeks, I realized that I was—ah—thinking a lot about her. She was still in Bunco, and I realized that I was making excuses to see her, talk to her. In other words, I was hooked. So . . ." As if he were admitting to something shameful, he dropped his eyes. But, doggedly now, he continued:

"So we went out after work to that Chinese restaurant on Harrison—the Jade Palace—and we talked. I told her where I stood—which is living with Ann and paying child support for my two kids in Michigan. She told me where she stood, which is being a single mother to a teenager named Charlie, and no child support from her no-good ex-husband. Also, she helps support her mother. So . . ." With the hard part over, Hastings drew a deep breath, spoke with an air of finality. "So after a couple cups of tea and a couple of potstickers, we decided that, even though we'd like to get it on, we wouldn't do it. We made the decision reluctantly. Very, very reluctantly."

Friedman permitted himself a small smile before he said, "That's a remarkable story, Frank. Really. It—Christ—it reads like an old-fashioned novel. I admire you. Janet, too. Of course . . ." The smile widened slightly. "Of course, where it's all going to lead, virtue over libido, that's something else. But for now"—he glanced at his watch, then pushed back his chair—"but for now, we've at least cleared the air. Which was, after all, the purpose of the exercise."

Also pushing back his chair, Hastings smiled ruefully. "Some exercise. I'm glad I'm not paying the check."

"Hmmm."

9

About to rise when Janet Collier entered the office—a gentleman's conditioned response—Friedman caught himself and merely nodded cordially as he gestured her to a chair at the opposite end of Hastings's desk. Hastings was also smiling, watching her move, as she placed a half dozen manila file folders on one corner of the desk. Today she wore pleated twill slacks, utilitarian leather shoes with lug soles, a turtleneck, and a light doeskin leather jacket, thigh-length. The jacket was buttoned over the nine-millimeter Glock semiautomatic she carried holstered at the small of her back. She would also be carrying handcuffs, a pager, ten spare rounds of nine-millimeter solid-points, and the tiny surveillance radio newly issued to all inspectors. As always, she wore her dark brown hair in a ponytail. No lipstick, no eyeshadow. No fun and games. She had knocked on Hastings's door at two o'clock, exactly the time of their meeting.

"So," Hastings said, smiling at her. "How'd it go, today?"

"You were right," she said. "Carpenter wanted to talk. Badly. As soon as he got into the car, on the way to the morgue, he started to talk—and talk. It was like we were the last two people on earth, honest to God. If I'd thought, I would've brought a wire, just so I wouldn't forget any of it." As she spoke, her dark, vivid eyes came alight with excitement. Hastings realized that she was experiencing the same quickening he'd felt working his first case from its inception. Like Janet, he'd only been in Homicide for a few months. A rapist had killed a teenager in the parking lot behind a four-screen movie house at the southern end of town. Hastings had been the first detective on the scene, making him the officer of record. And, yes, at the end it had been his collar, too: a sixteen-year-old straight-A student who heard voices. One of the voices was his dead father's. Another was a neighbor's Rottweiler.

"Suppose you start at the beginning," Friedman said.

Collier nodded, opened the topmost manila folder, withdrew a pad of yellow legal paper. Hastings caught a glimpse of her handwriting. Predictably, he thought, the writing was small and precise.

"I got to Carpenter's place about nine thirty this morning," she began. "He was all dressed, ready to go. He said he hadn't slept all night. He looked terrible, very thin, bad complexion. Those skin blotches—" Impatient with herself, she shook her head. "I can't remember the name, but it's typical of AIDS. Carpez syndrome, something like that. I'll look it up, before I start writing my report." She looked at Friedman, in a perfectionist's apology. Friedman shrugged, nodded, flipped a casual hand.

"We'd no sooner got in the car," she continued, "than he started in on his life story. He was raised in New Canaan, in Connecticut. His father was in advertising, a big shot. His mother, I gather, was very social. There was a lot of money. The father made a lot, and the mother inherited a lot. Randy was an only child and was mostly raised by nannies. His father worked in New York, where he kept an apartment. According to Randy, both his parents played around, had a series of love affairs. The three of them took separate vacations, he kept talking about that. His mother would go to Bermuda, or wherever, maybe to meet a man, and his father'd go to Europe. Randy, meanwhile, went to camps—all kinds of camps. He was very bitter about that—summer camps, ski camps, sailing camps. Anything to get rid of him. Plus, of course, boarding schools, where he'd mostly stay at the school over Christmas."

"Poor little rich kid," Friedman said.

"Exactly. And the other kids—his classmates—never liked him. Apparently when he was still very young—nine, ten years old—it was pretty clear that he was homosexual. Meaning that his classmates made his life miserable.

"Apparently, though, he was good at drawing and painting. His father started as an art director, in advertising, so maybe it was genetic. Anyhow, when Randy was in prep school, he started to get serious about art. Then he went to college and majored in fine arts. By that time, I think he'd come to terms with his homosexuality. Meaning that I think he came out when he was in college. Or anyhow, he had a few homosexual experiences."

"You say he came out when he was in college. Does that mean that his parents knew he was gay?"

"By that time," Collier said, "Carpenter's parents had divorced and both had remarried. His mother, in fact, remarried twice. I don't think they cared what he did. His father's secretary sent him a check once a month, and that was it. His mother lives in Switzerland. Or maybe it's Sweden." She frowned at her notes, shuffled the sheets of yellow legal paper.

"It doesn't matter," Hastings said. "We'll be talking to him again." He gestured. "Go ahead. Let's finish this."

She glanced at him sharply. Was it a rebuke? Or well-meant guidance? His smile suggested the latter. But with Friedman watching, she must not return the smile.

"When he got out of college," she said, "he lived in Europe for a year or two. Then he came to San Francisco. He became a commercial artist—illustrating, graphics. He went to work for an art service and did very well. I think he was happy for the first time in his life. San Francisco was the place to be, for homosexuals. It still is, of course."

"Except," Friedman said, "that about half the populace hates the gays. Among which populace, more than likely, there's the guy we're looking for."

"What about Charles Hardaway?" Hastings asked. "Did Carpenter talk about him?"

"Oh, God, yes." Her voice weighed heavily with sympathy. "It was heartbreaking."

"When I talked to him," Hastings said, "Carpenter told me that Hardaway had been married. He had a child."

She nodded. "His ex-wife's name is Doris. She lives in Detroit. There's a son, too—eleven years old. And Hardaway had a sister." Once more, she riffled the Yellow Pages. "Helen. She's thirty-something, and lives in Los Angeles. She's a social worker. Carpenter called her after we left, and she's coming to San Francisco today or tomorrow. Apparently she was very sympathetic to her brother."

"How about Hardaway's parents?" Friedman asked. "Have they been notified?"

"Helen will call them, Carpenter says."

"How old was Hardaway?"

"Thirty-five. He was a draftsman." She recited the names of his employers, past and present. "According to Carpenter, he was good at what he did. Very conscientious."

"According to Carpenter," Hastings said dryly, "Charles was perfect. Beautiful, too."

"God." As if to acknowledge defeat, an admission of guilt, Friedman shook his head. "I have to admit it. I can't—" For once at a loss, Friedman shook his head in bafflement. "I just don't understand how two guys can—" He broke off, glanced at Janet Collier, shook his head.

"It's companionship," Janet said. "Everybody needs somebody." As she said it, she avoided Hastings's eyes.

Hastings pointed to the manila folders. "What else've you got?"

She opened a folder that contained clipped-together sets of documents. "Hardaway's bills, mostly," she said. "And some ads, clipped from magazines. They have a very elaborate sound system, and a lot of the ads are for stereo equipment. Also bank statements and check stubs, plus statements from three mutual funds. There's an address book, too."

"Have you returned the originals to Carpenter?" Friedman asked.

"Not yet. There hasn't been time. Besides, I wondered whether, legally, Hardaway's sister—Helen—should have them."

Hastings unclipped his sheaf of papers, found copies of bank statements for the past three months. The statement for the month just past carried a balance of more than three thousand dollars. Next came bank-card statements from Visa, Discover, Chevron, and Texaco. Both the Visa and the Discover cards carried sizable running balances in three figures. The Chevron balance was almost two hundred dollars.

Also studying the documents, Friedman said, "Looks like he owed about as much money as he had in the bank."

"Look at the bank balance for February," Collier suggested. "Look at the deposits."

Hastings flipped the pages, found the statement. On the third and the sixteenth of the month, there were deposits of $1,183.40, obviously salary checks.

On the eighteenth of the month, and again on the twenty-third, Hardaway had made identical deposits of seven thousand five hundred dollars.

On the twenty-fifth, three checks for five thousand dollars each had been written.

"In March, just the two salary checks were deposited. But now look at April," Collier said. "Last month."

During April, Hardaway had deposited two salary checks, plus two deposits of five thousand dollars. In addition to miscellaneous checks drawn on the account during April, there was a round-number check written for ten thousand dollars.

"Anyone giving odds that those four big deposits were for cash?" Friedman asked.

Thoughtfully, Hastings riffled the pages before him. "So Charles Hardaway had something going on the side, it looks like."

"Twenty-five thousand in three months." Friedman, too, riffled pages. "That comes to a hundred thousand a year. Plus his salary as a draftsman."

On a notepad, Hastings doodled the numbers: 7500— 7500—5000—5000.

"All even amounts," he mused. "Very neat."

"There's more." Collier opened another folder, waved a sheaf of financial documents. "He had three mutual funds. There's one money-market fund, one stock fund, and one bond fund. And, yes, deposits in the three funds correspond exactly to the four round-number checks we're seeing in his account."

Friedman turned to Hastings. "Do you think Randy Carpenter would know if Hardaway was selling drugs?"

"I think he would," Hastings answered. "The feeling I got— their apartment—it was all shared. Everything suggested they knew all about each other."

"It could be," Janet Collier said, "that the money came from Hardaway's family."

Dubiously, Hastings shook his head. "I don't think so. Not according to what Carpenter said last night. No way."

For a moment, the three sat in silence. Finally Friedman said, "So what we've got, maybe, is drugs. Which would be a built-in motive for murder, never mind gay-bashing. Hardaway burned someone, and got killed."

Hastings pointed to Collier's file folders. "Give me the originals. I'll take them to Carpenter. That'll be a good excuse to talk to him again."

"Do you—" Collier hesitated, glanced covertly at Friedman before she asked Hastings: "Do you want me to come with you?"

Also glancing at Friedman, whose gaze studiously avoided them both, Hastings shook his head. "No. I want you to work on Hardaway's bank account. Those big deposits—were they cash, or checks? Don't let the bank jerk you around. The branch manager can get the information in an hour. They don't like to do it—turn over records without a court order—but they can." He glanced at his watch: almost three o'clock. "You'd better get on it." He gave her his card, the one with his home phone number. It was a reflex, part of the procedure. Only when she took the card, and he saw her expression flicker, did he realize the significance of offering her the card—an entrée into his private life. His life, and Ann's life. But he'd trapped himself; he could only go forward, play out the hand: "Call me at home, if it's after six."

Brusquely, he turned to Friedman, who pointed to a spare set of documents as he said to Hastings, "Why don't you tell Canelli to work on Hardaway's address book? The entries are pretty sketchy. You know—'Bob' and a phone number. 'Mechanic,' 'Cleaners.' But there might be something. You know—like 'CC' and a number. For 'Crack Connection.' "

"Right. Tell Canelli to come in, will you?"

Friedman nodded, left the office, raised a finger to Canelli, who was seated at his desk in the glass-walled squadroom. When Canelli acknowledged the signal, Friedman pointed to Hastings's office. As Canelli got to his feet and began walking toward them, Hastings spoke to Janet Collier:

"Remember, call me. We'll compare notes."

"I'll remember." She didn't look at him as she said it.

10

Carpenter shook his head. It was a sharp, peevish gesture. "I don't understand what you're saying." His dark eyes were hot, feverish with denial. "Are you saying that Charles was a—a crook? A criminal? Is that what you're saying?"

"Not at all." Hastings pointed to the documents stacked on the coffee table between them. "All I'm trying to do is clear up some inconsistencies. According to his bank statement, Hardaway received a total of twenty-five thousand dollars over a three-month period—in addition to what I assume was his regular salary. He also had three sizable mutual funds. Whenever we see money like that, especially in connection with a crime, then we need to have some answers. Where'd he get that much money? What'd he spend it on?"

Carpenter sat on a red velvet and walnut sofa, facing Hastings on a matching antique loveseat. The small living room was turn-of-the-century Edwardian, painstakingly restored. The furniture matched the vintage decor: antiques and pseudo-antiques, plainly expensive. It was a characteristic of gay couples, Hastings believed, that they lavished money and care on their surroundings.

Finally Carpenter spoke: "You're saying—implying—that Charles was in something illegal." With obvious effort, Carpenter raised his haggard gaze to make direct eye contact. "Is that it?"

"Are you familiar with Charles Hardaway's finances, Mr. Carpenter?"

"Not really. We kept separate, financially. We didn't have joint bank accounts, nothing like that. The first of the month we paid the household bills, and that was it. We've taken several trips together. He always had plenty of money." The bony shoulders lifted, a disclaimer. "That's pretty much all I know."

Hastings drew his notebook from an inside pocket, riffled the pages, finally found the right entry.

"Last night," he said, "you gave me a pretty concise rundown on Hardaway. Born in Detroit, went to college, married early, had one child. A few years later, he—" Hastings hesitated, then ventured, "He came out. Then he moved to San Francisco—here, to the Castro. He got a job as a draftsman. Is that right so far?"

Carpenter nodded reluctantly. He knew what was coming:

"He moved in here," Hastings said, "about three years ago."

"Right."

"Since then he worked as a draftsman. Correct?"

Exhausted, Carpenter could only nod.

"Last year, he made—what—twenty-five thousand, as a draftsman?"

"More likely thirty thousand, maybe thirty-five."

"But, if his bank statements are any guide, he was actually bringing in maybe a hundred twenty-five thousand a year. Maybe more. Maybe a lot more."

No response. Only the haunted, hollow eyes, staring down at the Oriental rug.

"So the question is, where'd the extra money come from? Not from his parents, it doesn't sound like."

"No." In the single word, Hastings could clearly hear a lifetime of bitterness. Whose lifetime? Hardaway's? Or Carpenter's?

"I understand from Inspector Collier that your parents are quite wealthy."

Carpenter's pale lips twisted in an embittered smile. "That's right, Lieutenant, they *are* quite wealthy. Unhappily, I have no contact with them. Both of us—" As if he were suffering a spasm of physical pain, Carpenter broke off, began shaking his head. But, doggedly, he forced himself to go on: "Both of us, Charles and I, were orphans, in effect. It so happens that, yes, my parents are rich. And it so happens that Charles's parents are working class. But, in both cases, we were embarrassments to them. So they cast us out."

"Charles had a wife."

"Yes. But they're divorced, long ago. Charles was an embarrassment to her, too."

"He had a child."

"His wife married a lawyer. They've managed to keep Charles away from his son. That was the hardest, for Charles. That's what embittered him the most."

"Charles's sister." Hastings consulted the notebook. "Helen. What about her?"

"I called Helen after you left. She lives in Los Angeles, and she's flying up this afternoon. She'll make the funeral arrangements. It's necessary, you see, that a member of the family make the arrangements." He sat silently for a moment before he said, "Helen is a social worker. She's very—very understanding. Very nice, really."

"Do you have any brothers or sisters, Mr. Carpenter?" Hastings spoke quietly.

"No," the other man answered. "There's no one. Except for Charles, there's never been anyone."

11

"But it's *done*." Billy, age fourteen, waved both hands vehemently. "I keep *telling* you, we got out at two thirty, because they canceled assembly. I was home by three, and I started right in. Besides, I only had homework in math and civics. And I—"

"Billy—" Ann drew a deep, disciplinary breath. "It's not the homework that concerns me. You're done early, I'm glad. But the point is, I just don't think you should be riding the Fillmore bus. I don't think—"

"But Tim's mother'll bring me home. I already *told* you that. If I get there, she'll bring me home."

"Tim, I'm sure, has homework. He—"

"Well of *course* he's got homework," came the plaintive response. "But I'm trying to *tell* you, we had a short day, because of the assembly. And I'm also trying to tell you that Tim did his homework when he got home, just like me. So—"

Dan, age seventeen, broke in: "How come they canceled the assembly?" As he spoke he spooned a second helping of rice pilaf onto his plate. The older boy's movements were smooth. If Billy was the volatile one, Dan was the thoughtful, deliberate one.

Exasperated, Billy ignored the question. At elevated stridency, he spoke to his mother: "How about you drive me? I'll do all the dishes before we go, and—"

"Billy." Her voice was firm, her expression grimly set. Privately, Hastings had labeled this Ann's schoolmarm manner, hard as nails. She taught fourth grade in public school. She knew all the tricks. "It's an hour, round trip. And I've got papers to correct. Lots of papers. So you—"

Harmonically, the telephones warbled: the primary phone in the living room, an extension in the rear bedroom of the huge Victorian flat, and a portable phone that could be anywhere.

"I'll get it." Quickly, Hastings put his napkin aside, walked into the living room, caught the phone on the second series of rings.

"It's Janet Collier, Lieutenant."

"Yes . . ." He turned his back on the archway leading to the dining room. Responding to her voice, he could feel the center of himself suddenly go hollow, an evocation of adolescence, that terrible time of uncertainty, of constant doubt.

"Is this a good time?" she asked.

"It—" He cleared his throat, began again: "It's fine. No problem. What've you got?"

"It's Hardaway's bank deposits. The big, round-figure deposits, they were all in cash."

This time, his visceral response was more complex. The imperatives of sex differed from the pleasure of an educated guess that had worked.

"Do the withdrawals correspond to the deposits?"

"Right down the line," she answered promptly. "In every case, the withdrawals followed the deposits by just a few days. And they all were checks that went right into the mutual funds."

"What about before the time covered by the statements we have?"

"Ah . . ." In her reply, he could clearly hear her excitement. "Ah—that's where it gets interesting."

"So are you going to tell me?"

"Our documents went back to February," she answered promptly. "Three months. Right?"

"Right."

"Well, the three months before that was a carbon copy, practically. Twenty-five thousand in big cash deposits plus salary checks. Fifty thousand in cash during a six-month period. And all the cash deposits are less than ten thousand dollars. Which means that the bank wasn't required to report them for money laundering."

"What about the rest of the year?"

"I checked over the past twelve months and it looks like the big cash deposits started just six months ago," she said.

He considered, then decided to say, "You did a good job. It's not easy, I know, getting access to bank records."

"Thank you." It was a formal answer.

"What we need now," he said, "is to get a handle on Hardaway. What kind of a person was he? How about his work record? Who'd he hang around with besides Carpenter? We know Carpenter has AIDS. What about Hardaway? Was he HIV-positive? What'd he spend his money on? We know he just bought an expensive car. What else did he buy? Maybe he had a sailboat. Or an airplane—who knows?"

"Do you want me to work on it tonight?" she asked. "That bar—Toby's—where Hardaway was last seen. Maybe . . ." Her voice faded. The message: she really wanted to spend the evening at home with her young son.

"Tomorrow's fine. You should get some sleep tonight. Tomorrow, plan on checking at Hardaway's place of business. Then make Toby's, the neighbors, whatever you can find."

"What about Carpenter? Will you talk to him?"

"Yes. The sister—Helen—and Carpenter, I'll do them tomorrow morning."

"What about the address book? Anything?"

"Not until tomorrow. This is Canelli's bowling night. He's running the addresses." As he spoke, Hastings turned, looked into the dining room. Dan was clearing the table, his assignment for the week. Then he would serve dessert. On his side of the table, Billy was sulking. Ann was holding her temper. Grimly.

"I'd better hang up," Hastings said. "I'll see you tomorrow at the Hall."

"Right." A pause. Then, in a more personal voice: "Good night."

"Good night." He, too, paused a meaningful moment. "Sleep well." As he spoke, he realized that he'd spoken loudly enough for Ann to hear. Involuntarily, his eyes sought hers as she sat at the dinner table. With both hands, she was twisting her napkin cruelly. Pain had darkened her eyes, tortured her mouth, drawn the muscles of her face taut.

Signifying that Ann knew.

For weeks—months—he'd suspected that she knew. A word, a glance, a quick flick of silence—all of it had confirmed that, somehow, Ann knew he'd fallen in love with another woman.

12

Instinctively deferring to the dominion of death, Hastings knocked discreetly. A moment later, on a night chain, the door opened just enough to reveal a woman's face. It was a pale face. The eyes were dark and anxious, the mouth was thin and grim.

"Helen Hardaway?" As he spoke, Hastings let his leather shield case fall open to reveal the badge. "I'm Lieutenant Frank Hastings. Homicide."

"Oh—yes. Just a second." The chain rattled, the door came open. But, rather than invite him in, Helen Hardaway stepped forward into the hallway. As she closed the door to her brother's apartment, she whispered: "Randy's sleeping. He's exhausted. Can we talk here in the hallway?" She looked anxiously up at him. It was a mannerism, Hastings suspected, that was characteristic of Helen Hardaway. Never quite sure of herself, anxious to please, she would often look up into the faces of others, hopeful of approval.

Hastings surveyed the small, meticulously decorated foyer before he said, "My car's at the curb. Let's talk there."

"You mean in a—" Apprehensively, she blinked. "In a police car?"

Almost laughing outright, he said, "It's an unmarked car, Miss Hardaway. Cross my heart."

"You're making fun of me." But she was smiling. The smile transformed her face, erased the anxiety, revealed a new dimension of warmth and insight into herself. This woman, Hastings decided, could be trusted. He gestured for her to precede him down the thickly carpeted stairs. Helen Hardaway's body was thick but not fat. She moved with a curious rolling gait, the movement of her shoulders and buttocks suggesting a denial of femininity. Was it possible—probable—that Helen Hardaway was a lesbian? She wore a sweatshirt, jeans, and incongruous fuzzy pink slippers. Her dark brown hair was close-cropped. Across the back of her sweatshirt the logo read, EUCLID WAS RIGHT!

"So you're two years older than your brother."

"Yes." Helen Hardaway nodded gravely. Repeating: "Two years." She spoke as if she were pronouncing a benediction—or a eulogy. They'd been talking for almost a half hour, sitting in the unmarked car with its radio turned off. Hastings had been content to let her ramble, dwelling almost entirely on the childhood she'd shared with her brother, both of them emotional refugees from the tyranny of a vicious father and a cowed mother.

"I was in my twenties," she was saying, "when I first learned about Charlie—about his sexuality. I was sure it had been my fault. I was a mousy little girl. I don't think I had three friends all the while I was in elementary school. So I'd con Charlie into playing with me. Sometimes I—" She broke off, bit her lip. Her eyes were focused far in the past, dim with remorse: "Sometimes I'd dress Charlie up in my mother's cast-off clothes, and we'd play house."

Hastings decided to say nothing in response, decided not to look at her.

"I used to laugh at him," she said finally. "He could never walk in Mom's high-heeled shoes. He'd always fall down. And I'd always laugh. He used to get furious." Smiling wistfully now, she shook her head. "Poor Charlie."

"Did you see much of him during the last few years?" Hastings asked.

"Two or three times, no more."

"You live in Los Angeles."

"Yes."

"When was the last time you saw your brother, Miss Hardaway?"

"I guess it was February, almost three months ago. I'm a social worker. Family planning. There was a conference in San Francisco, two days, in the middle of the month. Charlie and I had lunch."

Three months ago . . . In his mind's eye, Hastings reconstructed Hardaway's bank statements, and the cash deposits. Was it possible that the money had come from Helen Hardaway, who had carried it from Los Angeles? Was it possible that she and her brother had been partners in a drug business run out of Los Angeles? He stole a sidelong glance at Helen

Hardaway—and discarded the notion. Whatever else she was, Helen Hardaway was no drug pusher.

"When you saw your brother in February, how did he seem?" As he said it, Hastings privately winced. It was an awkward question. Too vague. Too naïve. He would have expected more from a rookie.

" 'Seem'?" she repeated. "In what sense?"

"Did he seem worried about anything?"

She thought about it, finally shook her head. "I wouldn't say he was worried, especially. But you should understand, Lieutenant, that Charlie and I weren't very close. Sure, I saw him only three months ago. Before that, though, it was more like two years."

"You kept in touch, though."

She shrugged. "Phone calls at Christmas, birthday cards, that was about it. We went through the motions."

"Was it his sexual preference? Was that it?"

"No." Sadly, she smiled, shook her head. "No, Lieutenant, it wasn't his sexuality. It was Charlie. He could be a real pain in the ass. He was vain and self-centered and petty. He could also be vindictive."

"That's not the picture I got from Randy Carpenter. He says he would've been lost without your brother to take care of him."

"Randy's dying. He's had to believe that Charlie was kind and true and generous. And who knows, maybe Charlie *was* wonderful to Randy. I hope so."

"How about Randy? What's your evaluation of him?"

"Randy's sweet," she answered promptly. "He's kind and generous. He's also very smart, and very sensitive. He's funny, too. At least he was funny before he got sick. When he was working—he was an illustrator—he came down to Los Angeles a lot on business. Sometimes he stayed with me, and we'd always go out to a restaurant. Great restaurants." Once more, sadly, she smiled. "I'll miss Randy. I'll miss him a lot."

"Was Charles HIV-positive?"

"I don't know. I don't think so."

"The drug they take for AIDS—AZT, I think . . . ?" He let it go unfinished, an inquiry.

"Yes. AZT."

"Does Randy take it?"

"I don't know. Why do you ask?"

Seated behind his cruiser's steering wheel, Hastings let his eyes wander idly down to the endless progression of tiny red lights blinking on the scanner mounted beneath the dash. This was his time for decision.

Finally he decided to say, "I ask about AZT because I know it's expensive. A hell of a lot more than an unemployed illustrator can afford."

"So?"

"So where'd he get the money, supposing he's on AZT? It doesn't sound like his parents would chip in."

"Are you saying that you think Charlie might've been getting the money? Is that what you're saying?" As she asked the question, her eyes widened incredulously.

There it was, his opening.

"In the last six months, Miss Hardaway, in addition to his salary checks, Charles has made bank deposits of fifty thousand dollars—all in cash, all rounded off. I'm trying to find out where that money came from—and where it went."

"Fifty *thousand? Really?*"

"Really. And that—"

"My God—" Awed, she turned to face him, her knee striking the barrel of the riot gun shackled to the floor between them. She muttered angrily, rubbed the knee. "You think someone killed him because of that money. Is that it?"

"It could be." He watched her for a moment, then said, "What d'you think?"

"What do I think?" Suddenly she guffawed. Repeating derisively: "What do I think?" Now her eyes were hot, angry. Good. Angry subjects often spoke before they thought.

"It wasn't a joke, Miss Hardaway."

"I know it wasn't a joke, Lieutenant. I'm not laughing out of merriment. I'm laughing instead of crying. Maybe it's because I remember Charlie trying to walk in those goddam high heels. Maybe I'm laughing now like I laughed then. Maybe—" Suddenly she broke off. She began to cry: dry, wracking sobs that shook her whole body. As a child might, she dug her fists into her eyes.

"Fifty thousand dollars," Hastings said. "What about the fifty thousand, Miss Hardaway?"

In reply, she shook her head sharply, a denial. About to touch her shoulder, an effort to comfort her, he hesitated, then withdrew his hand. For Helen Hardaway, the touch of his hand would not be welcome.

13

"There you are, Lieutenant." Canelli laid the accordion-folded printout pages on Hastings's desk. "The address book. All done." Canelli leaned back in Hastings's visitor's chair, crossed his pudgy legs, and watched anxiously as Hastings scanned the documents. Weighing in at a roly-poly two hundred thirty, Canelli bore a remarkable physical resemblance to Friedman. Their faces were similar: round and swarthy, with dark eyes and small mouths. But there the similarity ended. Almost never did Friedman's expression reveal what he was thinking, or feeling. In contrast, Canelli's face was a constantly running display of his inner self. Canelli was the squadroom innocent, the only homicide inspector in recent memory whose feelings lay so near the surface. Consequently, because he neither thought like a cop nor acted like a cop, Canelli had scored a remarkable string of successes. On the streets, it was as if Canelli were invisible to those whose livelihood depended on being able to spot a cop and act accordingly.

Hastings drew the printouts closer, scanned the pages: names, phone numbers, identifications. In less than half the entries, addresses were included. Occasionally an explanatory note was added. The first entry was Jerry Adams, 649-0250, followed by "picture framing." On a separate sheet Canelli had written in longhand: "147 entries, 8 unlisted. Pac Tel contact: Monica Gross," followed by a phone company number.

"You've been busy," Hastings said, nodding approval.

Canelli's reaction was a long, gratified exhalation. Once more, he'd managed to please. "Ah." He nodded. "Yeah. Thanks, Lieutenant. Anything new on the case?"

"I talked to his sister this morning. She said Hardaway was a real asshole."

"Did you tell her about that money?"

"Yes. She didn't have an explanation. It didn't come from her or her family, though, and she doubted whether Hardaway was involved in drugs." Hastings pointed to the printout of the address book. "Anything there?"

Frowning heavily, brow furrowed earnestly, Canelli shook his head. "Not that I could see. But I didn't—you know—dig into any of the entries. I mean, most of them are just 'Tom' and a phone number. And 'Tom,' even if the phone company adds 'Smith' to it, what've you got? I mean, it isn't going to be 'Tom Smith' and then 'Mafia,' or 'drug dealer,' or anything like that. How about Janet Collier? How'd she do at Hardaway's bank?"

"It looks like fifty thousand in the last six months. Cash. With corresponding withdrawals."

"Jesus . . ." Shaking his head, Canelli said, "That's a lot of money for a meek, mild-mannered draftsman."

"This morning," Hastings said, "when I talked to Helen Hardaway, I didn't get a chance to talk to Randy Carpenter, which I want to do now." He consulted his watch; the time was almost four o'clock. "While I'm talking to Carpenter, how about if you spend some time at Toby's?"

"Toby's? Is that—" Between Canelli's eyes, two lines of consternation appeared. "Is that the gay bar that . . ." Apprehensively, he let it go unfinished.

Anticipating an objection, Hastings nodded decisively, all business. "Right. Look, even though we'll obviously follow up on the money angle, this still might've been a gay-bashing after all."

"You mean—ah . . ." Canelli's face was a study in discomfort.

"If Hardaway was followed from Toby's, which is possible, then Toby's is obviously the place for us to start."

"Yeah. Well, I guess so. But—"

"After you've done Toby's, come back to the Hall. See if the computer comes up with anyone with a pattern of priors that fits. You know how it goes. Punch in gay-bashing, see what you get. When Janet Collier's finished with the bank stuff, tell her to help you out. The two of you can work together."

"Oh. Well." Plainly pleased, Canelli smiled. It was a shy, small boy's smile. In the presence of a desirable woman, Canelli clutched. "Well," he said again, "sure. That's fine."

"When you got the names in the victim's address book from the phone company," Hastings asked, "did you also get a record of Hardaway's billings for the past six months?"

"Yessir." Canelli pointed to a manila folder on Hastings's desk. "In there."

"Okay. You and Collier work on that, too. The phone company can give you the subscriber for every call."

"So—" Canelli cleared his throat. "So you want me to—what—spend a couple of hours at Toby's first. Then I go to work on Hardaway's outgoing phone calls. Is that it?"

"That's it. Problem?"

"Well, gee, Lieutenant, it's just that I—ah—I don't think I'll fit in, at Toby's. I mean—you know—someone's got to be a particular type, to—ah—" Once more, the other man broke off. His soft brown eyes were pleading for a reprieve. Causing Hastings to concentrate more closely on paper shuffling.

"What I mean is," Canelli began, "I don't—"

"This guy's been dead for almost two days," Hastings said. "Not only do we not have a clue, we don't even have a plan, not really. Got it?"

With deep reluctance, Canelli nodded. "Got it."

14

As Hastings was about to press the doorbell, the apartment door opened.

"*Oh.*" Startled, Helen Hardaway stepped back into the apartment. Then, relieved, smiling: "Lieutenant. Sorry."

"How're you doing, Miss Hardaway?"

As she'd done earlier, she stepped out into the hallway, closed the door behind her, lowered her voice: "My mother's flying in from Detroit. I've got to pick her up at the airport."

"Have you made funeral plans?"

"Tentatively. I wanted to see whether Mom would come."

"Do you think the funeral will be in San Francisco?"

"I'm sure of it. My father . . ." She set her mouth grimly, hardened her voice. "He wouldn't want it in Detroit."

Rather than reply, Hastings gestured to the closed door. "Is Randy awake?"

"He's pretty—vulnerable. But he's awake. Do you want to talk with him?"

"Please."

She turned, pushed open the door, called out: "Randy. Lieutenant Hastings is here."

From inside the apartment, Carpenter's voice was indistinct, disembodied: "Tell him to come in."

Hastings thanked the woman, entered the apartment. Just as he'd done on their two previous interviews, Carpenter sat on the antique sofa. His face was a death's head of despair. Perspiration beaded his forehead, streaked his face. His dark hair, lank and sparse, was plastered to his skull. Gripping the sofa's red velvet arms, Carpenter's hands were knob-knuckled and bony. The backs of the hands were blotched purple.

"I'm sorry to bother you again, Mr. Carpenter. But there've been some developments that I have to ask you about."

"Developments?"

"Yessir. You see—"

"Is it the money? Is that it?"

"Yessir, that's it. We—"

"Charles bought a twenty-thousand-dollar car. And other things, too. Charles had a taste for the good life. It's not a sin, you know." His voice was a wan, wasted monotone. There was no passion, no conviction. There was just the words, each word an effort.

"When we talked about that money, Mr. Carpenter, we were talking about twenty-five thousand over a three-month period." A pause, for emphasis. "Now we're talking about fifty thousand over six months—all of it cash. The deposits were in cash, none for more than ten thousand dollars. Which, as you may know, is the amount beyond which the banks have to screen cash deposits." Another meaningful pause. "The reason is drugs—the effort to turn up drug transactions. Money laundering, in other words."

"But—"

"Fifty thousand in the last six months, Mr. Carpenter. That's unexplained income. Unexplained and undoubtedly unreported to the IRS." Hastings broke off, watched the other man's face for a reaction. There was nothing. There was only exhaustion.

"The two of you have lived here for three years," Hastings pressed. "Is that right?"

Carpenter nodded: a bobbing of his head, supported by the loose yellowish cords of his neck.

"Answer the question, please." The command was clipped, framed in officialese. During their first two conversations, Hastings had deferred to this frail, sad man who had lost his lover—and who was about to die. But the city and county of San Francisco was paying him to find a murderer. Other municipal employees—social workers, doctors, nurses—they would collect their pay as they eased Randy Carpenter's passage from life to death.

"Three years," Carpenter answered. "Yes." Repeating: "Three years."

"Did you buy things together?" Hastings extended a hand in a gesture than included the small, elegantly furnished living room with its Oriental rugs and polished oak floors and a pair of museum-quality Chinese vases displayed on a black teak refectory table. "These antiques—your sound system—did you buy them together?"

"Some things we bought together. Some separately."

"You haven't worked for—what—a year?"

"A little less than a year."

"Meaning, I assume, that Charles Hardaway began picking up more and more of your living expenses. Maybe all of them."

For the first time, Carpenter's eyes sharpened, focused on Hastings.

"No," Carpenter said sharply. "*No.* I pay my own way."

"How?" Deliberately, Hastings spoke harshly, coldly. The time for compassion had passed.

"Th—" Momentarily the other man faltered. Then, with pale defiance: "That's none of your business, Lieutenant."

"Your parents? Family? Do they pay?"

"*No.*" Carpenter flared. Repeating vehemently: "*No.*"

"Do you take AZT?"

With the question, Carpenter's frail defenses began to fail. The exhaustion returned to his face; his voice dropped to a low, indistinct mumble as he said, "I don't have to answer that."

"You've already answered it, if you could see your face." Projecting a kind of reluctant pity for his victim, Hastings shook his head.

"There's nothing wrong with taking AZT." Now Carpenter spoke angrily, a flicker of defiance that quickly faded.

"Certainly not. But AZT's expensive. Very expensive, I'm told. I'd like to know where the money comes from."

"I don't have to—"

"It was Hardaway, wasn't it? He figured out some scam, to raise the money."

Carpenter began to shake his head doggedly. But now his eyes shifted, slid speculatively aside, then returned to engage Hastings. In that moment, transparently, there was a change. Until now, this moment, Carpenter had been telling the truth. He'd been too exhausted to lie.

Until now.

"It was Hardaway." Hastings spoke softly. On this moment, a knife's edge, the whole case could teeter. If he could gain the other man's trust, allay his fear, he could discover the truth.

"Tell me, Randy." It was both a plea and a command, both a request for help and an offer of help. "Don't let it all get dragged through the mud. You've got enough problems without that. Just tell me how it went, and I'll do everything I can for you. And for Charles, too. It's not like he didn't have a reason."

As Carpenter listened, he began to smile, a wry, ironic twisting of his pale lips. As if to taunt his tormentor, he began to shake his head, mimicking the same mocking pity that Hastings had offered him. "You're very good at what you do, Lieutenant. You're a lot more perceptive than you seem, I can see that."

"Thank you." Hastings's smile, too, was ironic, but he decided to say nothing more. Whichever way it went, here and now, win or lose, he'd done everything he could.

Finally Carpenter said, "I think you're an honest man, Lieutenant. I trust you. But I can't help you, about the money. Things we wanted"—he, too, waved a hand to encompass the room's decor—"we talked about what we'd buy. But we never talked about our bank balances. Never." The last word was spoken with grim finality. For a moment, Carpenter had wavered, about to confide in Hastings, about to tell the truth, tell what he knew.

But the moment had passed; Carpenter's face was closed now. Once more, truth had lost out to the lie, to expediency.

Acknowledging defeat, Hastings rose. On his feet, looking down at Carpenter, he said, "The AZT—did you pay for that? Was it your money?"

Carpenter nodded wearily. "My money. Yes."

"Are you going to tell me where the money came from?"

"No, Lieutenant, I'm not. Sorry."

"You might be making a mistake, not telling me. You realize that, don't you?"

"Yes, I realize that. Thank you, for warning me."

"You're welcome." Then, surprising himself, Hastings said, "Good luck."

"Thank you. And to you, too."

15

Walking slowly, Carpenter went to the front window, drew back the drapes. Yes, across Collingwood, Hastings was just swinging open the driver's door of an American sedan, certainly an unmarked police car. Appreciatively, he watched the detective's movements as he entered the car. In the vernacular, Hastings was a hunk, a pleasure to behold. Men like Hastings, so secure in their own aura of physical dominance, moved with a kind of calm, silky assurance that was all the more sensual because it was utterly unself-conscious. Hastings was a calm, quiet, confident man. Was he married? Certainly, once, he would have married. But now? Something in the detective's reticence, perhaps a protective device, suggested that Hastings was alone—looking, but not committing himself.

Sometime in the past, Hastings had been traumatized. Did he now march with the rest of them, the walking wounded?

Carpenter turned away, went into their bedroom. From the bookshelf, he took down the dog-eared paperback copy of *Catcher in the Rye,* turned to page 100. He sat on the bed, propped the book open. With the phone on the bed beside him, he touch-toned the area code, then the penciled number at the top of page 100: 824-4076. Three rings, and the connection was made:

"Yes?"

Mercifully, it was his voice. Not her voice. *His* voice.

"This is Carter." It was the code name they'd agreed on.

"Yes . . ." Conveying caution, yet also conveying warmth. He cared, then. Incredibly, he still cared.

"I wanted to tell you that—"

"Just a second." There was the sound of the phone being put down, followed by the sound of a door closing. Where, Carpenter wondered, was this special phone situated? In his study, his own private place?

"Yes. I'm back. How're you doing?" The depth of the voice, the modulation—the magic—all of it confirmed the bond between them.

"I have some bad news. Some terrible news, really."

"What is it?" Now, audibly, there was caution in the other man's voice. But, still, the warmth was there. The caring.

"It's Charles. He—two days ago, Tuesday, about eleven o'clock at night, he was killed. He was walking home from Castro Street, and someone killed him. Beat him to death."

"Oh, my God. Charles."

"Yes. Charles."

"I—I don't know what to say."

"I know. I shouldn't've called on this number. But I—I had to try. I had to tell you."

"Yes. Oh, yes."

Between them, a short silence followed. Until, speaking now more guardedly, the other man said, "We'd better hang up. Tomorrow, I'll send you a letter. Tomorrow, definitely."

"Yes. Thank you."

"I'm sorry. Very sorry, about Charles."

"Yes. I know."

"Do they know who did it?"

"No."

After another silence, the other man said, "This won't change anything. Nothing. You understand."

"Yes. I understand."

16

He carefully replaced the telephone in its cradle, pushed back his chair from the desk. But to what purpose? Did he intend to rise? Why? Certainly not to leave his study, this sanctuary of last resort. Here, now, he was safe. Here, now, he could decide what must be done—or not be done.

First, though, it was necessary to acknowledge whatever providence had timed the call to find him alone in the house. If, as Shakespeare had written, there really was a divinity that shaped one's ends, then this was his first proof of divine providence.

Charles, dead.

A beating, Randy had said. Death. Meaning that one potential problem was solved. Because Charles had questioned

Randy about their meeting. Ever since, Charles had tried to discover the secret they shared.

Charles, dead . . .

Was it murder?

Was it an execution? Could the labels be switched? Semantics. Word games. They were, after all, his stock in trade, divinities that would surely shape his ends, rough-hewn though they were.

Shakespeare, again.

Randy, alone . . .

Randy, soon to die.

Was Randy, now, the danger? Surely he would be questioned by the police. And Randy was fragile, delicate as the most exquisite flower. Even when he'd been young, laughing, so wonderful, Randy had been fragile. It was, after all, his charm. Delicate things were meant to be admired, not feared.

Until now, not feared.

17

"I've got to admit," Friedman said, "that, even though I still consider her a squadroom distraction because of that body of hers, the fact is that this Janet Collier does good work." He gestured to the printouts that covered much of Hastings's desk. "Look at that. This lady can make a computer talk to her."

Having learned long ago never to respond when Friedman admitted to a mistake, however benign, Hastings concentrated on a printout of the telephone numbers. For the past two hours, since 9:00 A.M., with the bank records already computerized, Janet Collier had been working with Canelli on calls made by either Carpenter or Hardaway. The printout listed the number called in the first column, and the name of the party called in the second column. The third column listed how frequently a given number had been called during the previous six months.

"I think," Friedman said, "that we should call her Collier. Not Janet, but Collier. I think that'd help."

For a moment Hastings was unable to make the connection. Then, when Friedman's meaning came clear, grateful for the thought, Hastings nodded. Saying: "I was thinking the same thing, exactly."

"Okay, then, let's do it. I'm not going to post a bulletin, obviously. But if you and I start calling her Collier, everyone else will fall into line. Hopefully."

"I agree."

"What you call her off duty, that's up to you."

Hastings frowned, hardened his expression, once more decided to remain silent.

"Okay." Friedman raised both hands, acknowledging another mistake. "Scratch that." He swept one hand over the printouts. "How're we going to proceed with all this? What'd Jan—what'd Collier find out at the bank? How'd Canelli do, on Castro Street? How'd you do, with Carpenter?"

"Jan—" Like Friedman, Hastings caught himself, began again: "Collier went back through a whole year of Hardaway's bank statements, but she didn't find any more big cash deposits."

"So what we've got," Friedman said, "is fifty thousand plus Hardaway's salary checks over a six-month period that ended with Hardaway's death. Period." He took off his heavy black-rimmed reading glasses, tapped them reflectively on Hastings's desk.

"Right."

"And your theory is that Hardaway got involved in some kind of a hustle that provided money to buy AZT for Carpenter."

"I'm not so sure it's a theory. Call it a possibility."

"But when you talked to Carpenter yesterday," Friedman insisted, "you had the feeling that he knew about Hardaway and the fifty thousand. He knew, but he wasn't telling."

"That was my impression."

"So the question is, why isn't Carpenter talking?"

Hastings nodded agreement. "Why indeed."

"When's the funeral?"

"It's this afternoon. Four o'clock."

"I'll bet," Friedman said, "that after the funeral, Carpenter will talk to you. This happens all the time, you know, after funerals. All the deceased's nasty little secrets come out. *Closure* is the with-it word. I well remember my uncle Morris. Not only was my uncle Morris able to stay out of jail despite the fact that he was an embezzler many times over, but he was also a world-class philanderer. Of course, none of this came out in Uncle Morris's lifetime, at least not in the full light of day. But then Uncle Morris died. And no sooner was he in the ground than everyone—*everyone,* including the grieving widow—unloaded. The point being that, once somebody's dead and gone, what's the point of making him look good? It's a relief to let it all hang out, tell the truth, for once."

"Okay, I'll question him."

Friedman shrugged. "What can you lose?"

"Nothing, except that talking to Carpenter depresses me. The poor guy's dying, and I don't think anyone really cares."

Friedman favored Hastings with a quizzical stare. "Since when do homicide investigators get to feel sorry for people?"

Resigned, Hastings nodded, gestured to the printouts. "Let's have Jan—Collier check out the phone calls."

"Jesus." Friedman riffled through the printouts. "That'll keep her busy."

"She can probably design a program—eliminate duplications and meaningless calls to the grocer and the auto mechanic, like that."

"Is the phone in Carpenter's name?"

Hastings shook his head. "Hardaway's, I think."

"How'd Canelli do frolicking among the gay guys on Castro?" At the image, Friedman smiled with pixie pleasure. "That, I would like to've seen."

"He put in a chit for almost thirty dollars this morning. Apparently he bought a round at Toby's."

"But no results."

"Not really. Everyone he talked to was very cooperative, he says, very glad to see the police on the job. But he didn't really get anything new. He—"

Hastings's outside line warbled. He excused himself, took the call.

"This is Farber, in the coroner's office. I'm new. Gregg told me to call you about the Hardaway homicide. We just finished him, but Gregg is running a little behind, and he asked me to call you."

"Fine. What've you got?"

"What we've got," Farber said, "is that Hardaway was HIV-positive."

Hastings nodded, told Friedman the news. Then: "Anything else? What about the murder weapon?"

"It was a club. A narrow club—a half-inch iron pipe, if I had to guess. The victim was hit hard enough in the stomach and again across the chest to break four ribs on the left side, plus the ulna of the left forearm, which was almost certainly a fending-off injury. He was also struck hard enough on the left side of the head to fracture the temporal bones."

"Was that the mortal blow?"

"No, sir, I don't think so. The mortal injury was a massive fracture at the back of the skull. That wasn't made by the weapon, we don't think. Gregg thinks the victim fell and hit his head on the curb. Gregg says the position of the body supports that supposition."

"So it sounds like a right-handed man wielding an iron pipe as he faced his victim. The victim fell backward, and hit his head on the curb."

"That's about it, Lieutenant," Farber answered cheerfully.

"Which," Hastings said, "corresponds with eyewitness accounts."

"Congratulations."

"What about toxicology?"

"Point four percent alcohol in the blood. Just legally intoxicated, in other words. No evidence of other drugs, no needle marks. In general, we've got a healthy, well-nourished, all-American male. If you don't count the HIV, that is."

"Okay, Farber. Tell Gregg thanks for the quick work. Send the report to my attention."

"It'll take a week at least, Lieutenant."

"No problem. And thanks again." Hastings broke the connection and reported the details to Friedman, whose response was mild exasperation.

"So what we've got," Friedman said, "is essentially nothing we didn't already know."

"Except that Hardaway had HIV."

"Hmmm." Friedman glanced at his watch. "It's almost noon. Lunch?"

Hastings shook his head. "I got on the scales this morning."

Friedman dismissed this with a snort and an affectionate caress of his considerable paunch. Then he heaved himself to his feet as he said, "Remember, after the funeral, go back to Carpenter. Results guaranteed."

"Hmmm."

18

Wearing the somber blue suit, white starched shirt, and black tie he'd worn for the funeral, sitting on his favorite vintage sofa, Carpenter had been speaking softly, with subdued precision, all animation drained away, all hope forsaken. Leaving only exhaustion. Once more, Hastings conceded, Friedman had been right. Randy Carpenter was vulnerable now. Vulnerable, and therefore compelled to talk, to unburden himself:

"When you know you're going to die," Carpenter was saying, "when you know you've got less than a year, then everything changes. Especially when you live in the Castro. Every time I go out, walk down to Castro, see the faces, it's like I see myself a few months from now in the various stages of my own disintegration." He paused, drew a deep, tremulous breath. "At the funeral, all the faces were there. I saw Dick Carroll, who could hardly stand up. Then there was Jack McCarville, who just found out he's got the virus. And then—" Suddenly he choked, sharply shook his head, fell silent again. As if begging for mercy, for release from the horror that only he could see, Carpenter raised both hands, a gesture of both desperation and supplication.

Even though he was aware of the pain it would cause, Hastings nevertheless had no choice but to inflict more pain. "They've done the autopsy," he said. "I just got the results this morning." He waited until Carpenter managed to raise his eyes. "Did you know that Charles had the HIV antibodies?"

"Ah—" As if he experienced a spasm of acute pain, Carpenter drew a sharp breath. His eyes were momentarily blanked out, as if he'd lost consciousness.

"I'm sorry," Hastings said. "I thought you would've known."

"I suspected," Carpenter whispered. "But I didn't know."

"You suspected but didn't ask. Is that it?"

"Yes . . ." Infinitely weary, Carpenter nodded. "That's it."

"Do you think Charles knew?"

There was no reply.

Studying the other man's face, sensing that this was the moment when Carpenter was most vulnerable, the make-or-break moment, Hastings leaned forward in his chair, softened his voice as he said, "You and I know that, the three times we've talked, there's always been something you've held back. Yesterday, especially, I got the feeling that you weren't telling me something about Charles that'd help me find his killer. Am I wrong?"

"No, Lieutenant, you're not wrong." It was hardly more than a whisper. Carpenter was sitting slack, his eyes closed, his head hanging loose, chin on his chest. For a long, silent interval the moment held, ever more taut between them. Then, still with his head low, eyes still closed, Carpenter began:

"It's been about nine months since I knew I had AIDS. I'd known I had the antibodies for about a year. In fact, Charles and I hadn't been together for much more than a year when I found out."

"Did you tell him?"

Deeply shamed, Carpenter shook his head. "No, not at first. I was afraid he'd leave me if I told him."

Hastings considered, then decided to risk asking, "Does that mean that Charles got HIV from you?"

Briefly, Carpenter roused himself, focused sharply on Hastings. "Not at all. The incubation period can be ten years, some say even longer. We were together for only three years."

"Ah." Apologetically, Hastings nodded. "Yes, I see. Sorry." He gestured placatingly. Repeating: "Sorry."

Acknowledging the apology, Carpenter nodded. Continuing: "You mentioned AZT when we talked yesterday. You seemed to feel that Charles had committed some crime so I could have AZT. Well . . ." A wan smile touched one corner of Carpenter's mouth. "Well, that's not the way it went, I'm afraid. It would be nice to think Charles was that altruistic. But it would never happen. Charles was sorry I'd gotten the virus, but that's as far as it went."

"But you did get AZT."

Carpenter nodded. "Yes, I got it. But it wasn't Charles who got the money. It was me."

"Ah . . ." Hastings nodded silently. This was the time to listen, not the time to talk.

"I worked for an art service—very nice people. I still do some illustrating for them occasionally. And they were as generous as they could afford to be, with a series of cash bonuses, over the past year. Unfortunately . . ." The small smile returned. "Unfortunately, the bonuses generated just enough income to make it impossible to qualify for AZT under welfare."

"What about your parents? Your family?"

The wan smile turned bitter. "My parents—they're divorced, and each remarried. They've turned their backs on me. At Charles's funeral, there were his mother and his sister Helen. I'm sure I won't be that fortunate."

"Your parents are rich."

"Yes, very rich. Self-centered, utterly vain. But rich."

"But they wouldn't help with AZT."

"If I asked them, I'm sure they'd help. But I would never—*never*—ask. I'd go without first."

"But you did get the money."

"Yes."

"Are you going to tell me about it?"

The smile began to widen. Slyly, Carpenter was enjoying the turnabout. Saying: "Yes, I'll tell you about it—to a point."

"Fine." Hastings returned the smile. And waited.

"As I've said, I was raised among the rich and the powerful. There was the waterfront mansion in Connecticut, the prep school in Massachusetts, an Ivy League college."

"Which college was that?"

Ignoring the question, Carpenter went on: "When I was in college, I acknowledged to myself that I was gay. I was very cautious, though. Back then, twenty-five years ago, Ivy League colleges weren't very accepting of homosexuality. I only had one very discreet affair. But that was enough. It put me in touch with myself, and I saw very clearly what I must do—

come to San Francisco, live among people who understood. And it was wonderful not to feel I had to conceal my sexuality. San Francisco's meant everything to me." Reflecting, he paused, momentarily lost in memories of happier days. Finally: "But then, a year ago, it all began to end. The only hope was AZT. Maybe AZT would buy time, enough time for a cure to be found. Wishful thinking, of course. They know now that AZT doesn't prolong—" He faltered. But, having begun the story, Carpenter was plainly determined to finish: "It doesn't prolong life. What it does, though, is make living easier."

"How long do you think you have, Mr. Carpenter? Can I ask?"

"I probably have three or four months." Carpenter spoke calmly, with dignity. His eyes were clear. From the effort the story cost him to tell, Carpenter was drawing strength.

"Ah . . ." With sympathy, and now a new respect, Hastings nodded. "Four months."

"When I tested positive for the virus," Carpenter said, "I had maybe five thousand in the bank, maybe less. I've never been good about saving, I'm afraid. But I wanted AZT. It was all I could think about. I was obsessed. But, as I've said, I was determined not to tell my parents. They'd hurt me too badly. So I started to think about alternatives." He smiled ruefully. "I even checked out the possibility of selling my body to a lab. Unfortunately, there's not much demand for AIDS sufferers. And the supply is increasing all the time." Once more, pain tore at Carpenter's desolate smile. "It's basic economics, you see. Supply and demand."

Hastings made no reply.

"So," Carpenter continued, "I had a problem. I wanted the AZT—needed it, I thought—but I couldn't pay for it. Charles didn't have the money—then. My parents were out of the question. So it was up to me. You can't imagine how desperate I was. In my mind, AZT represented life itself. It was a fallacy, of course, grasping at straws. But this is now, that was then. I was determined to do whatever it took to start on AZT. Once I'd decided, strangely enough, the solution was obvious." As if he were a teacher waiting for a student to respond, he broke off, eyeing Hastings expectantly. Again, Hastings decided to let silence work for him. Finally, with an air of finality, deeply resigned, Carpenter said:

"I suppose *blackmail* is the only word for it. Discreet, low-key blackmail."

When Hastings deliberately made no response to what was plainly meant as a revelation, Carpenter said, "Years ago—I won't tell you where or when—I had a brief affair with someone who, in later years, became very well known—and very, very wealthy. In his position, the nature of his work, it would be devastating to his career if the word got out that he'd had a homosexual relationship, never mind that it had been long ago and very brief. So I approached him—let's call him John. I explained my situation, and asked him to meet me."

"How long ago was it, that you approached John?"

"As soon as I knew I had AIDS. About nine months."

Hastings nodded, gestured for the other man to go on:

"Two days later, John came to San Francisco. We had lunch, and I laid it out for him. And he was . . ." Now Carpenter's smile was wistful, misty-eyed. "He was wonderful about it. Really wonderful. I hadn't seen him since—" He caught himself, then said, "It's been decades. Literally. But, God, it was one of those rare moments in life that works out wonderfully. I told him I had AIDS. He asked me if I had anyone to look after me. I said yes, even though . . ." He broke off. Plainly, the end of the sentence would have been, "even though Charles wasn't really reliable."

"John's next question," Carpenter said, "was money. Did I have enough? I told him I could squeeze by, probably, if I stayed close to home and didn't take AZT. For a minute or two, he didn't say anything. But then, Christ, he took out his checkbook, and wrote out a check for ten thousand. He'd take it out of petty cash, he said. And, since then, every month or two, there's a check in the mail."

"Before you go on," Hastings interrupted, "I'd like to know how you handled the checks."

Carpenter frowned. "I don't follow."

"Did you deposit them in the bank?"

Still frowning, Carpenter said, "I put them in the bank, of course. In my checking account."

"And you wrote checks against them."

"Yes. But—"

"Wait." Hastings's voice was sharp, edged with authority. "Just answer the question."

"The answer is yes. I put them in the bank."

"This was your own individual account. It wasn't a joint account, you and Hardaway." Once more, Hastings's voice was heavily weighted with authority, the full force of the law.

"No . . ." It was a slow, cautious answer. Repeating: "No. Just mine. We always had separate accounts."

"When you deposited the money in your account, did your bank ask you where you got the money?"

"No. I just deposited the checks by mail, no questions asked. It's not like I was depositing huge amounts, after all. Ten thousand or less, that really isn't much money."

"The checks you got," Hastings said. "Were they personal checks?"

Carpenter shook his head. "No. They were company checks—a real estate development company in LA. It was a front, John said."

Hastings took out his notebook. "Which company?"

"I—" Apologetically, Carpenter broke off. "I'd rather not say."

"We can find out, you know. You deposited the checks in your account. That's all we need to know."

Doggedly, despairingly, Carpenter silently shook his head. He was staring down at the floor.

"Are you still getting money from John?"

Carpenter nodded. "Yes, I am." There was an air of quiet defiance in the answer.

"In what amounts?"

"Between five and ten thousand."

Hastings switched tacks, hoping to catch Carpenter off guard. "In the past six months," he pressed, "did you ever see Hardaway receive any of the fifty thousand I told you about?"

"I—" Carpenter broke off, began to shake his head. Was it denial? Or a gesture of lost hope, of surrender? "I—" Once more, he broke off.

Hastings was aware of a deep visceral tightening. The trail had suddenly gotten warm. "You *did*. I can see it in your face."

With great reluctance, plainly deciding to gamble on the truth, Carpenter spoke slowly, gravely: "There was one time months ago—three months, at least. There was a messenger. He delivered a packet to Charles. And it was money—lots of money. I just caught a glimpse of it. But it was one of those big padded envelopes. And it was stuffed with money."

"And it was delivered by messenger, you say." At the center of himself, Hastings felt the excitement of the chase.

Carpenter nodded.

"You mean like a bike messenger?"

"He had a car. I was standing by the window, and I saw him get into his car and leave."

"Was there a sign on the car? A logo?"

"I think so. But I couldn't make it out. It was dark."

"But it was a regular messenger service. You're sure of that."

Again, Carpenter nodded. "Yes. Absolutely."

"Were there other deliveries by messenger that you saw?"

"One, about a month later."

"Was it the same messenger service?"

"I think so. But I'm not sure. Both of them came at night. Or, rather, evening, just after dinner."

Hastings nodded, took a long moment to study the other man. Were Carpenter's answers truthful? Could Carpenter be trusted?

Hastings decided to spar, shift his ground, watching for a revealing response. "Did Hardaway know John?"

Instantly, Carpenter stiffened. Saying sharply: "No. Absolutely not."

"You're very positive about that, Mr. Carpenter. You didn't have to think about it, not even for a second."

Defiantly, almost panting with suppressed anger, Carpenter refused to answer. His eyes moved evasively.

"They did know each other, didn't they? They—"

"If you persist with this, Lieutenant—if you keep poking around—you'll ruin whatever life I've got left. Do you understand me?"

"I can understand," Hastings said, "how you'd say that. But if you think I'm trying to ruin your life, you're wrong. I'm trying to find out who killed your lover. That's all I'm trying to do. So if—"

"Charles is dead and buried. If you really want to help me, you'll leave it at that."

"The thing is, I can't leave it at that. I wouldn't be doing my job."

"Your job." In the two words, spoken almost in a whisper, Hastings could hear the echoes of a lifetime lived in the shadow of society's contempt.

19

"This," Hastings said, "is absolute bullshit."

Aggrieved, Canelli nodded, then said, "With all the calling I did this weekend, this was one of the few services that wasn't helpful. I'll sure go out there to their office and lean on them, but—"

"Have you got their number?"

"Yessir." Canelli slid a sheet of paper across the desk, pointing with a pudgy forefinger. "It's Hermes Messages, and that's the number. And that's the manager. Carter, something. I never did get the first name."

Hastings touch-toned the number, waited for a woman's voice to say simply, "Hermes," then asked for the manager. In

9 6

the process of being put on a routine, bored-sounding hold, Hastings cut in sharply:

"I'm a lieutenant in Homicide, and I'm calling in the line of duty. I want to talk to Mr. Carter. Now. Right now."

"Well, if you'll just hold on, I'll see wheth—"

"What's your name?"

"It's Millie. But I—"

"If I don't talk to Mr. Carter in exactly thirty seconds, Millie, then I'm sending one of my detectives out there. And I guarantee he's going to make life very, very difficult for you people. Beginning with you. Do I make myself absolutely clear, Millie?"

Except for a click as the phone went on hold, there was no response. But only moments later:

"This is Carter speaking."

"I'm Frank Hastings, and I'm co-commander of the homicide squad." He recited his shield number. "I'm conducting a homicide investigation, and we're contacting every messenger service in town in the course of that investigation. Are you with me?"

"I'm with you."

"If we can get the information we need over the phone, it'll be very helpful, save us a lot of time. But when Inspector Canelli asked for your cooperation he didn't get anywhere—except to get put on hold. Are you still with me?"

No response.

"What I want," Hastings said, "is for you to tell me whether, in the past six months, you picked up any small packages and delivered them to Two-thirty-four Collingwood, apartment C."

"Do you have a name for the consignee?"

"Charles Hardaway."

"How soon do you need this information?"

"As soon as possible. An hour, let's say."

Grudgingly: "I'll see what I can do."

"Are your files computerized?"

"Naturally."

"Then we'll be calling you in an hour. And we'll be expecting some answers."

"Then you'd better let me get to it, Lieutenant." The line clicked, went dead.

Hastings cradled the phone as he asked, "How's Jan—" He broke off, began again: "How's Collier doing with the phone calls?"

"She's working her ass—" Canelli, too, broke off. Saying: "She's working like hell. I guess she's got a computer at home. Anyhow, she worked last night on the telephone calls."

"She's got a teenage kid, and she got a computer for him. So all she has to do is take a disk home with her."

"Yeah, well . . ." Canelli nodded approval. "Well, that's great. She—"

Hastings's telephone warbled, the interoffice line.

"It's Janet Collier. I've got the phone calls almost finished. I thought I should tell you."

"Ah." Spontaneously, he smiled, looked through the glass wall of his office out into the squadroom. At her desk, phone to her ear, Janet was smiling at him, nodding a greeting.

"Come on in," he said. "You and Canelli need to work out a plan."

"The phone-calls log—shall I bring it?"

"Certainly." He broke the connection, summarized the call to Canelli, who began to button his collar and draw up his tie.

"Never mind your tie," Hastings said. It was an order. "This is work, not dress-up."

98

"Oh. Well. Sure." Canelli's soft brown eyes were chastened. Hastings had hurt his feelings.

Overcoming the reflex to rise when a woman entered the room, Hastings gestured for Collier to take one of the two visitors' chairs, and find a spot on his desk for her file folders. There were two folders, one for printouts, one for notes taken on legal tablets in Collier's neat, even handwriting.

"So," he said, "what've you got?"

"The phone is in Hardaway's name," she said, "but they both used it. I went back six months, which was easier for the way the phone company keeps its records. The first thing, I entered all the numbers called. It came to almost three calls a day—two point eight, actually. Which, I guess, is probably about average. Then I eliminated the duplications, obviously. I gave the numbers back to the phone company, and they gave me the subscribers' names. If it was the corner grocery, or a ticket agency, whatever, I didn't contact them. The name was all I needed. That brought down the number I actually called to about sixty-five. So then I just started at the beginning, and tried to call every one of the sixty-five."

"Whew!" Canelli breathed. "It sounds like it'd take a week."

"I got pretty tired going through the whole spiel." She mimicked herself: " 'This is Inspector Janet Collier, San Francisco Police Department.' Half the people got defensive, and half thought it was a joke, or a scam. Several thought I was selling tickets to the Cops and Kids games. One guy came on to me, claimed he had a thing for lady cops. But eventually I got through the list, got their connections to Hardaway or Carpenter. I got a lot of answering machines, of course, so there're still some loose ends. Lots of loose ends, actually."

"How about unlisted numbers?" Hastings asked.

Anticipating the question, she nodded, consulted the legal

pad. "There were three unlisted numbers called. One was a plumber, don't ask me why. The other two, all I got was their machines." She flipped a page of the legal pad. "One was to a woman named Nancy Sloss, who lives in Arizona. The other was to a man named Delbert Gay, who's in San Francisco. I decided to—"

At the last name, Hastings's head had come up sharply; his gaze focused intently on Collier.

" 'Gay,' did you say? 'Delbert Gay'?"

"Right." Just as intently, her gaze focused on him. Now Canelli was avidly nodding in reaction to the name. Collier looked from one man to the other, saying: "Are you guys going to tell me?"

"Delbert Gay," Hastings said, "is a sleazy private eye." He swiveled his chair, took the San Francisco phone book from a narrow table behind his desk, turned to the Yellow Pages, turned to "Private Investigators." He found the two-line listing for "Delbert Gay, Since 1972." He looked at Collier, then read off the phone number in the ad. Promptly, she shook her head. The numbers didn't match.

"So the question is," Canelli said, "why would Hardaway or Carpenter call Delbert Gay on his private line?"

"How many times was the number called?" Hastings asked as he swiveled back to face the two inspectors.

"Just once," Collier answered.

"Did you check the numbers called against Hardaway's address book?" Hastings asked.

"Most of them."

"Was Delbert Gay in Hardaway's address book?"

"No."

"You're sure?"

"Maybe he'd memorized the number. Or written it on a calendar, or something." She shrugged. The lift of her shoulders elevated the swell of her breasts. Hastings looked away, then looked covertly at Canelli. Yes, Canelli had been admiring Janet Collier's bosom.

To Canelli, Hastings said, "You'd better go back to those messenger services. And you," he turned to Collier, "unless something else turns up with those phone numbers, you'd better work with Canelli. He'll fill you in."

"What about Delbert Gay?"

"I'll deal with Delbert Gay. We understand each other." Hastings looked at each of them in turn, then flipped up his hands. Staff dismissed. As he watched Canelli trying unsuccessfully to let Collier precede him out into the corridor, Hastings touch-toned the unlisted number for Delbert Gay. After four rings, Gay's voice said he was unavailable, leave a message. Next Hastings consulted Gay's listing in the Yellow Pages. He touch-toned the number, got another message. As Hastings was leaving his message, Gay's voice came on the line.

"Lieutenant Hastings? How's it going?"

"Fine, Delbert. How's business?"

"Steady, I'd say. Not bad, but not great. What can I do for you?"

"That homicide in the Castro last Tuesday. Ring a bell?"

"I heard about it, yeah."

"The victim was Charles Hardaway."

"Yeah . . ." It was a cautious response.

"Know him?"

"Not that I remember, Lieutenant. Why?"

"He lived with a guy named Randy Carpenter. Two gay guys. They shared the same phone. About three months ago, a call was made from their phone to your unlisted number. Remember that?"

"Would you give me those names again?"

Speaking slowly, deliberately, Hastings repeated the names.

"No," Gay answered, this time speaking decisively. "No. Sorry."

Hastings consulted the copy of the phone bill that Janet Collier had left him. "The date of the call was February fifteenth, at ten thirty at night."

"How long did the call last?"

Once more, Hastings scanned the bill. "Less than a minute."

"Sounds like it could've been a wrong number. Someone got the machine, and then hung up. Happens all the time."

"The billing address for your unlisted number is on Twenty-sixth Street. Is that your home?"

"Yeah—an apartment."

"In the Yellow Pages, there's only a phone number, no street address. Does that mean you're working out of your home?"

"You got it," Gay answered casually. "Keep down the overhead, it's the only way."

"So the billing address for your office phone would also be for your home."

"Right."

"And you're sure—absolutely sure—that you've never had anything to do with either Hardaway or Carpenter."

"Absolutely."

"This is a murder investigation, Delbert. If you lie to me, it's your ass."

"Have I ever lied to you, Lieutenant?"

"Definitely, Delbert. You know it, and I know it."

"I gotta protect my clients, you know. I've got to—"

"Remember what I said, Delbert. You lie to me, that's when your troubles start." He broke the connection.

20

Delbert Gay dropped a quarter in the slot, punched out the number, let the phone ring through eight times. At the ninth ring, a sleep-blurred voice said, "Hello?"

"Are you awake enough to listen to what I'm going to tell you?"

"Sure. What time is it?"

"Almost 10:00 A.M."

"So. I was up late."

"You know who this is."

"Sure," Hubble said.

"Okay. I'll only say this once. I want you to leave town. Go to Portland, or Seattle. Not Los Angeles. Remember, not Los Angeles. In a week, better two weeks, call me from a pay phone. Call me at the office."

"So there's a problem."

"I'm not sure. I don't think so, but I'm not sure."

"Two weeks—that'll take two thousand."

"Two thousand—okay."

"What about my stuff?" Hubble asked. "Stereos, like that. CDs. What about my CDs?"

"Make sure your rent's paid a month ahead, and leave your fucking CDs in the apartment. Pack a bag and split. Jesus." He slammed the phone onto its hook, looked quickly but carefully around the busy streetcorner. He'd chosen a phone booth at the intersection of Market Street and Dolores, only a few blocks from the Castro.

Gay took a slip of paper from an inside pocket, moved his lips as he memorized the number. He dropped another quarter in the phone, touch-toned the number. Waiting for an answer, he checked the time: ten minutes after ten on a bright, clear morning in May.

"Mr. Weston's office," a woman's voice said. The three words were smoothly modulated, an evocation of success, of muted power.

"My name is Robert Brown," Gay said. "Mr. Weston is expecting me to call."

"Just a moment, please."

Almost a full minute passed before Bruce Weston came on the line.

Because the name Robert Brown was a code word that meant possible trouble, condition yellow, Weston had only to acknowledge the message: "Yes. I understand. Robert Brown."

Then, with a forefinger that trembled slightly, Weston broke the connection. He remained seated behind his desk.

Never did he feel more secure, more in control, than when he was as he was now, in his quilted leather executive chair, both hands resting lightly on the exquisitely joined, variegated woods of his desk. He noted with satisfaction that, in this position, the cuffs of his gleaming white shirt extended a precise inch, enough to show the gold medallion cufflinks that were replicas of ancient Roman coins.

It was important, he knew, absolutely vital, that he not surrender to fear. In the chain of command, he was perfectly positioned, insulated both from the top down and also from the bottom up. If the police should call, he had only to say that he was following orders handed down by a client. However, lawyer-client privilege constrained him from revealing the identity of his client.

His sole mission had been to recruit Delbert Gay. He'd talked to Gay for less than a half hour. Then he'd handed over an envelope stuffed with money. He'd hailed a cab, and returned to his office. Safe. Until now, safe. And gratified by the certainty that he'd gotten his foot through the door and entered the world of Harold Best, and therefore of James Forster. For years—decades—Weston had aspired to Forster's world— and this was finally his opening. It was a milieu of pure power, a world so influential that money was never exchanged. Only favors, many of them discussed over hundred-dollar lunches that were never paid for directly, only signed for. Some men never carried cash, only credit cards. Men like Forster carried neither.

As always, whenever he ruminated on the circles of power he'd begun to penetrate, Weston felt soothed, focused. Accordingly, after drawing a long, deep breath, he instructed his secretary to hold his calls. Then, from memory, he touch-toned the Best campaign manager's private line.

The call was picked up between the second and third ring.

"This is Barton Sobel."

"Yes. Barton, this is Bruce Weston."

"Ah. Bruce. What can I do for you?" The question was asked calmly, without inflection.

"I've—ah—just had a call from Robert Brown."

There was a brief pause, then a slight but significant change of inflection as Sobel said, "How long ago?"

"Just now." Weston consulted his watch. "Ten fifteen. Five minutes ago. No more."

"Is it something you can't handle?"

"So far, no. But I thought I should call you, put you in the picture."

"Good—and you're on top of it." It was a statement, not a question.

"Oh, absolutely. I just thought I should pass it on. Keep you current."

"Of course. Thanks. Good-bye, Bruce."

"Good-bye, Barton."

21

Even at a glance, Hastings could see the excitement in Canelli's eyes. Walking behind him, Collier carried the inevitable manila folder and was smiling in spite of herself. In response, Hastings felt the warmth of anticipation, of restrained exuberance.

"Let me guess," Hastings said as his two inspectors sat across from him at his desk. "The messenger service."

Smiling broadly, Canelli nodded vigorously as Collier opened her folder. "You got that right, Lieutenant," Canelli said. "And guess *which* service."

Covertly, Hastings sighed. Among all the homicide inspectors he'd ever commanded, only Canelli played guess-who.

"Hermes."

Once more, Canelli nodded vigorously. "Right. How'd you know?"

"Canelli, we're wasting—"

"When you talked to Carter, at Hermes, you must've scared the sh—" He broke off, glanced uneasily at Collier.

"Were you going to say 'shit'?" she asked sweetly.

Predictably, Canelli began to blush. Collier smiled at him, plainly an expression of genuine affection. Working together, the two had become friends.

"So . . ." Hastings cleared his throat. "So what've we got?"

"What we've got," Collier said, consulting the documents in the folder, "are six messenger deliveries from Hermes to Hardaway during the past six months. Four of the deliveries were billed to Delbert Gay. But the first and fourth were billed to Weston Associates." She raised her eyes, stole a look at Hastings. Did the name ring a bell? He shrugged; the name didn't register.

And yet . . .

Hastings frowned, gestured for her to continue. "Weston is a lawyer," she said. "That's all I know. I decided not to contact him until I'd talked to you."

"I've heard of him, I think. He—"

"*Hey,*" Canelli interrupted. Repeating with enthusiasm: "Hey, I know him. I testified against some guy he was defending." Decisively, Canelli nodded. "Yeah. Bruce Weston. He does a lot of criminal work."

"That could fit." Collier tapped the sheet of paper that listed the Hermes pickups. "Bruce Weston is connected to Hardaway through Delbert Gay."

"How so?" Hastings asked as he reached for his own pad of legal paper.

"On the fifteenth of November, Hermes delivered a package from Bruce Weston to Delbert Gay. Two days later, Hermes delivered a package from Gay to Hardaway, followed by another delivery the following month. The next couple of months the same thing happened. After that, four packages went from Gay to Hardaway. So it's pretty plain what happened. Weston supplied the money to Gay, and Gay distributed it via Hermes. All the deliveries from Gay went to the Collingwood address. Probably Hardaway knew to contact Gay if there were any problems with deliveries. Which would account for the phone call from the Hardaway phone to Gay."

"And that one call could break the case open." Marveling, Canelli shook his head. "Isn't it amazing, how things work out?"

Once more consulting her list, Collier said, "The last delivery from Gay to Hardaway was about a month ago, in mid-April." She gestured with the sheet of paper. "I'll have copies made."

"That phone call to Gay from the Hardaway phone," Hastings said. "When was it made?"

"In February," she answered promptly. "Three months ago."

"What we need now are phone logs for Delbert Gay and Bruce Weston, see if they talked with each other." Hastings looked at Canelli. "Why don't you work on that, Joe?"

"Well, sure, Lieutenant. Except that—" As if to appeal the order, Canelli looked at Collier. "Except that Janet is so good with a computer, maybe . . ." He let it go unfinished.

"Sorry," Hastings said, "but I want to take Collier with me to interrogate Bruce Weston. She's the officer of record. If this is a break, with Weston, then she's entitled."

"Oh. Well. Sure, Lieutenant. I didn't mean . . ." Canelli turned his soft brown eyes on Janet Collier, smiling placatingly. Repeating: "Sure. No problem."

"Good." Hastings rose, locked his desk, and reached for his sport jacket, hanging on a clothes rack. Saying to Collier: "We'll take my car. Meet you in the garage in fifteen minutes."

"Fine." She, too, was on her feet, glancing at her watch. "I'll get Weston's address. Shall I call him, make an appointment?"

Hastings shook his head. "Let's surprise him. Get Delbert Gay's address, too." And to Canelli: "If you get lucky and establish a phone connection between Weston and Gay, call my pager."

"Yessir."

Hastings regarded Canelli for a moment of silence before he decided to say, "If you're ever going to take the sergeant's exam, Joe, you'll have to know about computers. You know that, don't you?"

"Yessir, I know that." Resigned, Canelli nodded heavily.

"Good."

22

"I hope," Weston said, "that we can wind this up in twenty minutes. Fortunately for you, I've had a cancellation." Tolerantly amused, Weston smiled. "Something about a poodle with a foxtail up his nose." The smile widened urbanely. "In this business, one learns to be flexible."

"I understand," Hastings said, "that you practice criminal law."

"Among other things. I also do personal injury and product liability. Torts, in other words."

"Do you have any partners?"

"No. There's just me and my secretary and two paralegals, plus one associate." The smile widened disarmingly. "I'm not very good at partnerships. I like to make my own mistakes."

Behind gold-rimmed designer glasses, blue eyes danced, an invitation to genteel repartee.

"Are you acquainted with Delbert Gay?" Hastings asked.

"Sure. He's a private investigator. I use him in criminal work. Protective coloration, as the zoologists say." Weston smiled again, this time in smug appreciation of the phrase he'd just turned.

"Meaning?"

"Delbert Gay," Weston said, "is pretty sleazy, let's face it. Which means that he fits right in with certain low-life types. That can be very helpful in criminal work."

"He looks like a crook," Collier said. "Is that it?"

Appreciatively, Weston turned his attention to Janet Collier. In his forties, impeccably groomed and supremely self-confident, with the body of a weight lifter and the slow, appraising smile of a singles-bar stud, Weston let a long, speculative moment pass as he stared at the woman seated across the desk.

"That's it exactly, Inspector. The raunchier the company, the better Gay fits in."

"What about Charles Hardaway?" she asked. Her voice was calm and measured, but her eyes were sharp-focused, her gaze locked with Weston's, probing, testing. "Did you know Charles Hardaway?"

Weston frowned, then shrugged. "Charles Hardaway?" Amicably, he shook his head. "Afraid not. Sorry."

"What about Randall Carpenter?"

"Are these people supposed to be business associates?" Weston asked. "Is that it?"

Ignoring the question, Collier repeated, "*Do* you know Randall Carpenter?"

"Wait a minute." Gracefully, Weston raised his left hand, a

gesture of restraint. On his pinkie, a star sapphire caught the morning light streaming through a large window that offered a view of San Francisco Bay, with the cityscape in the foreground and the Oakland Hills in the background. "Wait," Weston commanded. "Hardaway—was that the gay guy that was killed last week? Is that the Hardaway we're talking about?"

Rather than answer, Collier looked at Hastings, seeking guidance. Hastings let a thoughtful moment pass. Then: "That's the Hardaway, Mr. Weston. Did you know him, have any dealings with him?"

Instead of replying, Weston suddenly rose, turned his back, went to the picture window. He stood motionless for a moment, arms stiff at his sides. The silky fabric of his high-style Italian suit caught the pale blue light reflected off the water of the bay, and turned iridescent. As the silence lengthened, Hastings covertly turned to Collier. He smiled and winked.

How should she respond? Did they have Weston on the defensive, was that the meaning of the wink? It seemed possible. She decided to return a smile.

When Weston turned away from the window to face them, there was no trace of humor or good-fellowship in the lawyer's expression. Behind the designer glasses the blue eyes were cold.

"If you mean was Hardaway a client, the answer is no." Weston's voice, too, was cold.

"What about Randy Carpenter?" Hastings asked. "Was he a client?"

"No."

"But you know Randy Carpenter—know who he is."

"Why do you say that, Lieutenant?" It was a quizzical question, casually asked.

"Just answer the question."

Weston shook his meticulously barbered head. As if he truly

regretted the necessity to instruct Hastings in his duty, Weston spoke softly, superciliously: "I've got to remind you, Lieutenant, that I'm an officer of the court. Therefore, I'm not compelled to answer your questions."

"What about Hermes Messages? Is that a familiar name?"

"Lieutenant . . ." With condescending good humor, Weston shook his head. "Perhaps you weren't listening. I said that I have no intention of—"

"If you've nothing to hide, then why not tell me whether you use Hermes Messages?"

"We use messenger services daily. I have no idea what they're called."

"Six months ago, Hermes delivered one package from you, personally, to Delbert Gay. We have reason to believe that this package contained money that was subsequently divided up and distributed to Charles Hardaway at Two-thirty-four Collingwood." Hastings paused, watched the words register, watched Bruce Weston struggle to keep his expression aloof, genially disdainful, as he returned to his desk and sat for a moment in reflective silence. Finally, speaking with exaggerated patience, he said, "As I'm sure you realize, Lieutenant, lawyers perform a variety of services for their clients. It's quite possible, for instance, that one of my clients wanted to get money to someone. However, the donor didn't want to reveal his identity. The remittance-man gambit, in other words. In a case like that, the lawyer's job would be to preserve his client's anonymity."

"Let's suppose," Collier said, "that you have a client who's involved in drug smuggling. Let's suppose he uses you to make payoffs. He sends the money to you, and you use Hermes to distribute it. And let's suppose that our investigation leads us to you. Would you—?"

"Wait." Once more, imperiously, Weston raised his hand.

"First, you've got to establish what information my client gives me. If he tells me I'm handling drug money, then I'd be in possession of guilty knowledge. But if he merely tells me he wants a given number of packages distributed to certain people, no questions asked, then that's all I'm required to reveal. I might suspect my client's a drug dealer. But I'm not—"

"Suppose we told you," Hastings interrupted, "that you possess information that's important to a homicide investigation. And suppose you prevent us from getting access to that information."

The answer came quickly, decisively: "That question isn't for you to decide, Lieutenant. If you can convince a judge that I have information you need, and it's being withheld, then the judge might issue a search warrant. Otherwise . . ." Weston spread his hands, signifying his disinclination to pursue the conversation. Pointedly, he glanced at his watch. Saying apologetically, once more the smooth-talking lawyer: "I'm sorry I can't be of more help. But I've got to—"

"Do you mind if we talk to your secretary, Mr. Weston?"

"Oh, yes, Lieutenant, I mind very much. We're trying to conduct a business here. And I'm afraid you'll have to show cause before you make any further demands on me or my staff."

They were all standing now. As if on cue, Weston's phone buzzed discreetly, doubtless an interoffice call.

"That'll be my next client. Here." Weston gestured to one of the office's three tall wooden doors. "You can leave this way. Thanks for coming by, Lieutenant. And good luck with your investigation. If you turn up a suspect . . ." Weston offered an embossed business card. Hastings studied the card ruefully. Clearly, Weston had won every round—and meant the card as a memento of his victory, a smug mockery. Collier opened the door and left the office without a backward glance. Her body language expressed both frustration and anger. The door led to an outside hallway. Like Bruce Weston's office, the hallway was thickly carpeted, discreetly decorated, softly lit.

"That smug son of a bitch," Collier fumed. "He—the bastard was making fun of us the whole time."

"He's had his fun. Now it's our turn. Sure as hell we can connect him to Hermes, and to Delbert Gay. So now all we've got to do is connect Gay to Hardaway. Which, in a sense, we've already done, via Hermes."

Standing in the hallway, they were talking in low, hushed voices, breaking off whenever someone passed.

"A guy like Weston's always tough," he said. "They're part of the establishment, and they all play golf with each other. But the bigger they are, the harder they fall, once their buddies quit returning their calls. Believe me, I've seen it happen. I've landed bigger fish than Weston. Bigger and meaner."

"Meaner?" She spoke dubiously.

"Listen." He squared to face her, put his hands on her shoulders, to reassure her. Instantly, she drew back. Her eyes flashed. The message was clear: hands off during duty hours.

"Listen," he repeated, "you're making a mistake if you let someone like Weston run over you. Because he could be pissing in his pants, right this minute."

In spite of herself, she smiled. Skeptically.

"You've got to think about the facts. Forget about the sideshow Weston's putting on. That's all it is, a sideshow. The facts are that Randy Carpenter has admitted to blackmail. He contacted someone very rich, and threatened him with exposure unless he sent money. Which the other man did. Then there's Hardaway, who also got money. Which suggests to me that Hardaway was doing the same thing Carpenter was doing, and at the same time."

116

She nodded vehemently. "Yes. I agree. Completely."

"Maybe," he said, "they were blackmailing the same person."

She frowned. "But—"

"Let's assume Hardaway got killed because he was blackmailing Weston—or someone Weston represents. If that's what happened, then we've got to figure out how Weston managed the murder. Sure as hell Weston didn't beat Hardaway to death. He hired someone to do it. So the question is, who did Weston hire, and how did he hire him?"

"Are you going to put him under surveillance?" she asked. "Is that what you're thinking?"

He smiled ruefully. "Hell, I don't know *what* I'm thinking. I'm just noodling."

They'd been standing in the hallway long enough to attract glances from the curious among the constant stream of passing office workers and messengers, most of them waiting for the nearby elevators. Hastings stood with one shoulder resting against the marble wall beside him. In that position, he was aware that a young boy, ten or eleven, had left his mother's side as she waited for an elevator. Unmistakably, the boy was making for Hastings. The boy's eyes were fixed on Hastings's waist on the left side, where his holstered revolver bulged. Hastings pushed away from the wall, turned his back on the boy, and spoke to Collier: "Carpenter is the key. If he tells us who he was blackmailing, then the case breaks wide open."

She nodded. "I agree."

"I've talked to Carpenter several times. I think he's a nice guy, and I feel sorry for him. In some ways he's actually very cooperative, very forthcoming. But, so far, he's made it very clear that he's not going to give us the name of the guy he was blackmailing. And I don't see any way I can muscle him.

What'm I going to threaten him with? Imprisonment? Death?"

"I know . . ." Collier, too, had turned her back on the boy, who now stood close by, staring steadily at them.

"So . . . ," Hastings said, "you want to give Carpenter a try?"

Her eyes widened. "Me? Just me?"

Pretending diffidence, all business, Hastings shrugged. "It's like I said, I've run out of moves. It's your case. See what you can do." He glanced at his watch. Time: almost eleven thirty. "See you at the Hall at four o'clock. Okay?"

"Yes—fine. I appreciate this, Fr—" Quickly, she caught herself and corrected: "Lieutenant."

"Good luck." They turned toward the elevators, where the small boy's mother now held him firmly by the hand, her eyes on the blinking numerals above the elevators. Hastings smiled at the boy. There was no response, only a dark, solemn stare. On impulse, Hastings palmed his shield case, showed his lieutenant's shield. Instantly, the boy smiled. In that same instant, the boy's mother jerked him into the newly arrived elevator.

"Big shot," Collier chided.

"Public relations. Didn't you read the chief's latest memo? When in doubt, smile."

"So. I'm off. Right?"

He nodded. "Right."

"Any orders?"

"Just use your own good judgment. You know what we need. Lie, cheat, I don't care, do whatever it takes to find out who he's blackmailing. Threats, promises, sweet talk—try it all."

"What about you?" she asked.

"I'm going to see what Delbert Gay's got to say."

They entered the crowded elevator. Self-consciously, they stood shoulder to shoulder. They did not speak.

118

23

"Jesus, Lieutenant, what can I *tell* you? I mean, sure, I worked for Weston—him and I bet twenty, thirty other clients, the last six months. Mostly it was neck-brace stuff, like that, for Weston. I mean, let's face it, he uses maybe a half dozen investigators besides me. And the big-ticket gigs, he gives them to someone else."

"You use Hermes Messages. Right?"

He shrugged. "Yeah, sometimes."

"Starting last November, you had Hermes deliver small packages to Two-thirty-four Collingwood periodically. Right?"

Delbert Gay spread his hands, a pantomime of innocence. "Hey, Lieutenant, that was months ago. You can't expect me to remember—"

"Ah, but I can, Delbert. You know I can. You know what'll happen if you jerk me around."

"Aw, come on, Lieutenant, when've I ever jerked you around?" Gay spoke plaintively. He was a big, overweight, untidy man in his fifties. Sparse ginger hair fringed a freckled pate. His complexion was improbably ruddy, with a network of broken capillaries across his nose and cheeks. His voice was thin and reedy, a chronic whine. Because his stomach was so large, Delbert Gay habitually sat on his spine, stomach up. His suits always needed pressing, his run-over shoes always needed shining. His hair was in constant disarray. He sat behind an outsize oak desk that was piled high with papers.

"Just so we understand each other," Hastings said, "I'll lay it out for you. We've got Charles Hardaway on the take, maybe very high-level blackmail. We've got Weston tied to Charles and you. Then we've got you tied to them. Got it?"

Gay half-nodded, then shrugged.

"No—no." Hastings shook his head. "You remember how it goes, Delbert. Nodding, shaking your head, that's no good. You've got to answer." Hastings smiled mocking encouragement. Saying sweetly: "You remember."

"Okay   sure . . ." Gay shifted from one bulky ham to the other, at the same time waving pettishly. Like his head, Gay's hands were freckled, tufted with ginger-colored hair.

"You see where I'm going with this, I imagine," Hastings said.

"Yeah, I see," Gay said bitterly. "You're setting me up, that's where you're going. You got nothing from Weston, so now you're coming down on me."

Genially, Hastings smiled. "As a matter of fact, you're absolutely right, Delbert. I figure I can squeeze you, really hand you the shitty end of the stick. Hell, I can put you out of business for ninety days, just by telling a judge I've got reasonable cause for impedance of justice in a capital crime. Let's say that's the way it goes, and you get a ninety-day license suspension. Okay?" Hastings mocked the other man with a bogus smile.

At the thought, Gay winced visibly, as if he'd experienced sudden pain.

"I figure," Hastings said, "that after a week or two on suspension, you'll tell me what I want to know."

No reply. Behind his desk, Gay sat in a black vinyl and chrome executive chair. The quilted vinyl, Hastings saw, had been cut in two places, and was trailing white cotton batting. Gay's watery eyes were blinking as he stared down at the cluttered desk. His mouth was small, compressed between plump, pneumatic cheeks. His Cupid's lips were an unhealthy purple. Gay was beginning to breathe heavily, audibly wheezing. His mouth was slightly open. His eyes had turned furtive.

Finally, with obvious effort, he raised his gaze to meet Hastings's steady stare.

"What is it that you're looking for?" Gay asked. "Exactly?"

This, Hastings sensed, could be the beginning of Gay's capitulation—the break. All the indications were there: the uneasy eye movement, the fretful fingers, the suggestion of quickened breathing as the blood began to pump faster, suffusing Gay's broad, plump face, already chronically flushed. All of it combining in an unmistakable aura of fear.

Delbert Gay was cracking.

"What I'm looking for," Hastings said, "is the truth. The whole truth. Everything, whatever you know about Charles Hardaway—the way he lived, and the way he died."

Once again, Gay's eyes had dropped to his desk. His plump fingers began toying fretfully with a foot-long chain of paper clips that lay on his desk. The chain might have been prayer beads. When he spoke, it was in a soft, clogged monotone:

"You probably never knew it, but I've had a heart problem for years. All the weight I'm carrying, I know that's the problem—the weight, and the booze, that don't help, either. But then, a few months ago, Christ, I end up in the hospital, and it turns out I got cancer. Liver cancer, the worst kind. And—" He blinked ruefully, shook his head. "And I have to tell you, Lieutenant, it shook me up. I mean, let's face it, the truth is, there's no one out there gives a shit whether I'm alive or dead. My ex-wife drank herself to death. I got two grown kids somewhere—a boy and a girl, with kids of their own. But the last time I heard from either of them, it was a Christmas card from my son, maybe five years ago. There wasn't even a return address. Which really pissed me off. No return address, I mean. What kind of shit is that?"

In silence, Hastings watched the other man's descent into despairing self-pity. Still fingering the chain of paper clips, Gay's hands were trembling. At the corners of each eye, tears were glistening.

"What I hate," Gay said, "is maybe having no one come to my funeral. I hate the idea of just being dropped in some goddam potter's field somewhere, like garbage."

"You can find your kids," Hastings said. "Christ, that's your business, finding people."

Gay's small, pursed mouth twisted into a stricken counterfeit of a smile. "Oh, sure, I guess I could find them. But then what? We're going to fall into each other's arms, is that what you think? And then I say, 'Oh, by the way, I'll be dying in a month or two. So you wouldn't mind taking care of the funeral expenses, would you?' "

"Maybe we can work something out, Delbert." Hastings

spoke quietly, reflectively. "I'm not promising anything. But I could look into it, see what the people upstairs say. There's a lot of favors owed us, you know. Undertakers, the coroner, we do business with them all."

Almost shyly, Gay raised his watery eyes. He studied Hastings for a long moment. Then he ventured: "You think it could work, Lieutenant? No shit?"

"All I can do is try, Delbert. That's all I can do. No promises. The only thing is, you've got to go first. You'd have to trust us, that's the only way it'd work."

"Sure . . ." Gay was staring at nothing—deciding. Then, dropping the paper clip chain and clearing his throat, he said, "I been doing odd jobs for Bruce Weston maybe two years, something like that. One of the jobs was using Hermes to make deliveries, all kind of deliveries, just so my name was on the chit, not Weston's. Okay, so I was a cutout. But, what the hell, the pay was good, and I wasn't breaking any law. That's one thing about Weston. He pays good.

"So then, a few months ago, give or take, he said he wanted me to check out the guy on Collingwood I'd been making payments to. Weston said that the guy had to suffer, feel some pain. You know, have his leg broke, something like that. Did I have somebody who could handle the job? Well, hell, you know I *did* have somebody. But I didn't come right out with it. I stalled. I mean, I wanted to see how serious Weston was. So then he says, okay, I can think about it, but in the meantime he wants me to get a look at the guy. So then, maybe a month later, Weston and I meet downtown, on a park bench. He says he's just heard from his client, and Hardaway is getting to be a problem that's got to be dealt with. Weston had money with him—ten thousand dollars. He says I can split it up any way I want. I can hire someone, or I can do the job myself, whatever.

Well, I'd been expecting it, and I had a couple of questions. Like, is Hardaway supposed to know why he's getting worked over?"

"How'd Weston answer that?"

"He said no, nothing fancy, no conversation. Just break the guy's leg, whatever, then split, don't talk. Hardaway'll know what it's all about, he says. So then I said what if something goes wrong, and Hardaway dies? Weston just shrugged. Either way, he said. But the pay's the same."

"He said that? Either way? You're sure?"

"Absolutely sure."

"So what'd you do?"

"I called up a guy named Claude Hubble. He's a young black guy, twenty-three, twenty-four, no more. Mean as hell. But he's also smart, always makes sure the back door is open, like that. And he's very particular about details. I spent maybe a week staking out Hardaway and made sure Hubble knew Hardaway by sight. I even called Hardaway once, to set up a delivery. That was so Hubble could see Hardaway up close."

"You called Hardaway?"

"Right. But all I got was a machine. So finally I had to leave my number, and he called me."

"On your unlisted phone."

"Yeah . . ." Speculatively, Delbert Gay's eyes sharpened. "You knew that, eh?"

Hastings made no reply.

"My unlisted phone—you got it from the phone company."

"I'm a cop, Delbert. Remember?"

"Hmmm." It was a petulant rejoinder.

"What happened then, Delbert?"

"What happened was, I turned Claude loose, told him the

job was on, any time he wanted. And, Christ, he couldn't wait, it turned out. He did it the very first night. I had the feeling he liked the idea of working a fag over."

"How'd you pay Claude off?"

"Five hundred before, five hundred afterwards."

"Did it bother Claude, that Hardaway died?"

Gay shrugged. "Not that I could see. These guys, some of them, they see so many guys get killed, it doesn't bother them. Sad, but true."

"Where can I find Claude?"

Wheezing, Gay leaned forward across his desk, scribbled on a notepad. "That's his phone number."

Hastings glanced at the number. "Where's this?" he asked. "Hunter's Point?"

Gay shrugged. "I guess so, but I don't know for sure. That's something else about Claude. He's careful. He's mean as hell, isn't afraid of anything. But he's careful. Also, he could be running. I called him yesterday, told him you guys were looking for him."

Pocketing the slip of paper, Hastings said, "So it didn't shake Claude up, that he's on the hook for murder?"

A small, wet guffaw erupted. "Not Claude. Nothing shakes him up. Besides, he hates the faggots. Really hates them. That's why he did the job so quick."

"What'd he use? What kind of a weapon?"

Gay raised his beefy shoulders, shrugging. "He didn't say, and I didn't ask. If you knew Claude, you'd know what I mean."

"After Hardaway was killed, did you contact Weston?"

"Just once. I called him from a pay phone."

"What was the conversation? Weston could fall for murder one. What'd he say?"

"He didn't say anything. He just said thanks, very polite, and hung up. A couple of weeks before, he gave me a code name. Robert Brown. If I called him, told him I was Robert Brown, he knew there was trouble."

"What kind of trouble?"

Resigned, Gay spread his hands. "This kind of trouble."

"So you called him, with the Robert Brown name."

"Yeah."

"When was that call placed?"

"Yesterday, about ten in the morning. I—"

At Hastings's belt, his pager beeped. He pressed the button, read "649-0250. Collier." Hastings wrote the number beneath the number for Claude Hubble, then turned to Gay: "I'd like to make a couple of calls, Delbert. How about if you step out for a cup of coffee. Give me fifteen, twenty minutes. Then we'll finish our business."

"Sure." Laboriously, Gay got to his feet, gestured to the phone. "All yours."

Hastings waited for the office door to close, then touch-toned Collier's number. She answered immediately: "I think Carpenter's ready to talk. He wants you included, though. He wants assurances." In her voice, Hastings could hear the excitement, the pride. She'd done her job.

"Does he know who had Hardaway killed?"

"I think so. Or, at least, he suspects."

"What made him decide to talk?"

"I think it's a delayed reaction to Hardaway's murder. At first, he was numb. Now, though, with the funeral behind him, he's getting mad. He wants to see justice done."

"Where're you phoning from?"

"A sidewalk pay phone in the Castro."

"Does Carpenter know we're talking?"

"Yes."

Hastings checked the time: twelve thirty. His stomach was rumbling. "I've got to call Friedman. Suddenly this thing is breaking wide open. Delbert Gay gave me a name for the assailant. I'll put it in the works. Then I'll get some lunch. Let's meet at the one hundred block of Collingwood, and walk up to Carpenter's. How about one thirty, an hour from now?"

"Fine. I've got to eat, too."

About to suggest they eat together, a natural suggestion, Hastings caught himself. He could predict her reaction: nothing personal during business hours, no grounds for gossip.

"Okay. One thirty." He broke the connection, put through a call to Friedman. He recapped his conversation with Delbert Gay, then repeated what Collier had just said.

"My God," Friedman said, "twenty minutes, and the whole case makes. Every Tuesday morning should be like this."

"It's mostly that both Carpenter and Delbert Gay are dying," Hastings said. "They want to get straight."

"Delbert Gay . . ." In Friedman's voice, Hastings could hear the familiar easygoing irony. "It won't be the same without Delbert to kick around."

"So," Hastings said, "you're going to collar Claude Hubble. Right?"

"Right. I'll put Canelli and Marsten on it. Sigler, too, maybe. What about Carpenter and Gay?"

"I'm going to meet Jan—Collier—in an hour, and we'll talk to Carpenter. Then I'll bring Gay down to the Hall. That should be about three o'clock."

"Do I understand that you've actually promised Gay a deal that includes a *funeral?*"

"I said I'd try. If it doesn't work out, who's to know?"

"He doesn't have any family?"

"A son and a daughter. But they're estranged."

"Jesus, Carpenter's estranged from his family, too. That's how this whole thing started, when you think about it. Carpenter's family rejected him years ago. And look what's happened."

"You'd better see about Claude Hubble. He could be running."

"Right. See you about three."

24

"I'll give you the name," Carpenter said, "because I suspect Charles died trying to blackmail the man who was giving me money. Charles saw it work for me, and he decided to try it. That's why he died, I think."

"Are you worried that you could be attacked, too? Is that why you're talking to us?" Hastings asked.

Carpenter shook his head. Today, he was dressed in sandals, blue jeans, and a light wool plaid shirt. If possible, he looked closer to death each time Hastings saw him. Carpenter was sitting in his favorite red velvet sofa.

"No, I'm not worried for myself. I guess I just want to know what happened. I want to know what Charles did—when, and for how long, for how much. I also want to know who ordered the attack on him." He broke off, frowning, perhaps perplexed. Saying finally, reflectively: "Maybe, bottom line, that's what I really want, to know who had him killed."

Hastings glanced at Collier, who questioned him with her eyes. Did he want her to take a turn? Almost imperceptibly, Hastings shook his head. Now, they would wait.

Carpenter's eyes, too, were in motion, silently searching the faces of the two detectives who had first come to him as the enemy, interlopers. But they had persisted, finally to share with him this final decision.

The silence lengthened, palpably weighing on each of them. Until finally, with infinite reluctance, Carpenter began to speak:

"Harold and I were in college together—the same fraternity. We were much different, Harry and I. Harry was golden, one of those wonderfully attractive, inherently charming people that everyone wanted to know, to be with, laugh with. I was always quiet, introspective. Harry laughed his way through. I worried.

"No one suspected that Harry was gay. Whenever the occasion demanded, Harry would arrive with a beautiful, adoring girl on his arm. I think I might've been the only person in school who knew about Harry. We were very careful, Harry and I. We only made love twice. Both times, it was in our senior year, after a keg party at the frat house.

"Harry married after graduation. Of course, she was beautiful, and talented, and her father was enormously wealthy. Her name was Carolyn, and she came from Los Angeles. Her father—James Forster—owns vast tracts of agricultural land in the Central Valley. He also owns a few office buildings in Los Angeles, plus a shopping mall. Harry went to work for his father-in-law. Of course, he did wonderfully. He worked hard, and he has a world-class smile. Everyone wants to be Harry's friend, especially when they realize James Forster is his father-in-law.

"For a wedding present, Forster gave the happy couple a mini-mansion in Bel Air. He also gave them memberships in the best country clubs. In other words, James Forster controlled their lives. Completely. Apart from the making of money, which he considered banal, Forster's entire life was centered on his daughter. Whatever Carolyn wanted, even as a child, Forster encouraged her to go after. And, by God, she got it. Not always because she was James Forster's daughter, but because Forster had taught her which strings to pull, who she could buy off, who she couldn't. And the more she got, the more she wanted. Not money, that didn't interest her except as a tool. Society, so-called"—Carpenter shook his head—"she couldn't care less. What Carolyn wanted was what her father wanted. Power. Anonymity and power, those're his passions. Her passions, too."

"What kind of power?"

"Political power, of course. In California politics, in Forster's party, nothing happens without Forster's approval. It's impossible to get a campaign off the ground unless he gives the word. He probably contributes more than a million dollars a year of his own money to political campaigns. And he influences the gifts of millions more."

"My God," Hastings said, "I don't think I've ever heard of him."

"That's the point," Carpenter said. "That's the way Forster wants it. A lot of rich, powerful men pay people a lot of money to keep their names out of the papers. James Forster is one of them. Forget Donald Trump and Ted Turner. They're the grandstanders. It's men like James Forster and Warren Buffett and Daniel Ludwig who really pull the strings."

"So," Collier said, "how do we get from James Forster to you—and Hardaway?"

"Harry," Carpenter said cryptically.

"Harry?"

"Harold Best." Having pronounced the name, Carpenter let himself sink back against the cushions of his sofa. His eyes were only half open; his breathing was shallow, his face pale. Against the pallor of his skin, the blotches that marked it were a dark, engorged red.

"Jesus," Hastings said, turning to Collier. "Harold Best." And to Carpenter: "He's the one, then. Harold Best. Your—your friend from college. He's the one you called when you needed money."

Wordlessly, Carpenter nodded. Shame was clearly etched in his pallid face—shame and regret and something else, infinitely tender. Was it love?

"So what's the rest of it?" Collier pressed. "What's the whole story?"

"The rest of it?" Carpenter asked, his voice quizzical. As if the story no longer interested him, he smiled ruefully. "The rest of it was pretty predictable. Inevitable, really. Harry's star began to rise. He was good at his job, and his forehand was first class. And, yes, about ten years ago, at age thirty-seven or so, he started running for things—the school board, councilman, then the state senate. It was an inevitable parlay. His wife gave him the game plan, told him what he would do. His father-in-law provided the money and the connections. As the years passed, Forster realized that he'd finally found the perfect candidate, right in his own family. Harry had it all—the looks, the smile, the wit. Best of all, though, Harry lived in perfect harmony with his limitations. He was smart enough to take orders, but not so smart that he began getting ideas of his own. Which, for Forster's purpose, was perfect."

"So now," Collier said, "Harold Best is running for the United States Senate. The election is"—she counted on her fingers—"it's six months from now."

Wearily, Carpenter nodded. "Yes."

"And Best is still sending you money."

"Yes. He's glad to do it, I think. I'm sure of it, in fact."

"How did it go?" Hastings asked. "Start at the beginning. You called Best, and told him you had AIDS. Then what?"

"Then Harry came up here, to San Francisco. We had lunch—a long lunch. We told each other about ourselves. It was wonderful, really—twenty-some years that just dropped away. It was as if we were transported back in time to those careless days at college. We were so innocent, then. Life was so wonderful. So—" Suddenly Carpenter's voice caught; there were tears at the corners of his eyes. For a long moment, no one spoke. Then, heavily, Carpenter shook his head. The magic of memory had faded, leaving only the harshness of the reality.

"But then Charles found out about the lunch, and he demanded an explanation. Of course, I had to tell him the whole story."

"You told him everything?" Hastings asked. "The money—you told him Best would send you money?"

"I didn't have a choice. Charles could be very jealous. And he had a terrible temper."

"So," Collier said, "it all started over the lunch with Harold Best. He promised you money. You told Hardaway. And that's how it all started."

Carpenter looked at her, a speculative glance. He made no reply.

"Hardaway knew you'd be getting money from Best," she pressed. "And he knew *why* you'd be getting the money. He saw a chance to line his own pocket, go into business for himself."

Carpenter nodded. It was a painfully remorseful nod, heavy with regret.

"Did you know Hardaway was blackmailing Best?" Hastings asked.

"No. I had no idea. None. Not until he was dead, and you were asking questions."

"Did Best ever discuss it with you, tell you Hardaway was blackmailing him?"

Carpenter shook his head vehemently. "You don't understand. I only saw Harold once—the lunch. After that, except for the checks, there was very little contact between us. It was because of his campaign—I had to stay away from him, you see. Because of the publicity."

"The phone—did you talk on the phone?" Collier asked.

"Sometimes."

"But the money. Did he ask when you needed more money?"

"Yes. He knew when to ask. And he was very generous."

"How generous?"

As if it were a shameful admission, Carpenter mumbled, "It came to about five thousand a month."

"Five thousand for you, and twice that for Hardaway," Hastings said. "More than twice."

No response. Carpenter sat in a posture of utter dejection, head bowed, shoulders slumped.

"So," Hastings said, "until Hardaway was killed, and we got a look at Hardaway's bank balance, you had no idea Hardaway was blackmailing Best. Correct?"

Carpenter nodded: a loose bobbing of his head on a scrawny, corded neck.

"Even when Hardaway got killed," Hastings said, "you didn't suspect anything."

"I thought it was a gay-bashing."

"What would you say if I told you that we think we know who killed Hardaway?"

"You—" Carpenter blinked, focused sharply on Hastings. "You know?"

"We think we've got the assailant's name, and we think we know who hired him. We think it was a private detective based in San Francisco. We suspect that a local criminal lawyer gave the detective his orders."

"Will you be talking to Harry?" Carpenter asked. The question was put hesitantly. Plainly, he dreaded the inevitability of Hastings's response:

"We don't have a choice, Mr. Carpenter. We've got to talk to Mr. Best. You can see that, can't you?"

"Oh, God . . ." Hopelessly, Carpenter began to shake his head. Repeating: "Oh, God."

25

"Harold *Best*?" Incredulously, Friedman shook his head. "Our next senator? *That* Harold Best?"

Amused, Hastings nodded, glanced sidelong at Collier. When had he last seen Friedman caught off balance, surprised? Always, Friedman sought to stay ahead of the curve.

Enjoying the moment, Hastings nodded. "That's the Best."

"You don't think it's all part of some con, do you?"

Hastings frowned. "How do you mean?"

Friedman shrugged. "Maybe Carpenter'll tell Best we're on his trail. 'But don't worry,' Carpenter'll say. 'The cops can't do anything without my testimony. And I won't testify against you. Provided, of course, that you send lots more money.' "

Decisively, Hastings shook his head. "That's not Carpenter." He looked at Collier, for confirmation. She nodded vigorous agreement.

"I realize," Friedman said, "that you guys like Carpenter. You'll recall, though, that this whole thing started when he began putting the arm on Best. You'll also recall that we're only six months from the elections. If it gets out that Best is—was— gay, he's finished. He's history."

"If Carpenter exposes Best," Hastings mused, "and if Best has to drop out of the Senate race, then Carpenter cooks his own golden goose. Why should Best go on paying to protect his image once he's exposed?"

"Hmmm." Speculatively, Friedman eyed Hastings. Then: "So you have confidence in Carpenter's story. You're willing to go down the line with it. Both of you." Friedman tested Hastings's conviction with an inquisitor's gaze, then turned his eyes on Collier. Finally, drawing a deep breath, he said, "Okay, I'll buy it. Let's not forget, though, that going after someone with Best's clout is a very, very big step. So let's be very, very careful." And to Collier: "How about if you give us a few minutes?" He smiled, moved his head toward the squadroom. Returning the smile, she nodded, gathered together a sheaf of manila folders, and left Hastings's office.

"What we've got here, for God's sake," Friedman said, "is a major problem in diplomacy. I guess you know that."

Hastings nodded. He knew.

"I mean, not only are we going after Harold Best, our next senator, but we're also going to tangle with his wife, who's supposed to be very, very tough. Not to mention his father-in-law, who's supposed to have more money than half the countries in South America. And who regards people like us as serfs."

"Serfs?"

"Pawns. Whatever. The point being that, in California,

James Forster anoints the politicians who make the laws. If he doesn't like the laws, he buys himself another batch of politicians."

"I didn't know you were into politics."

"I'm fascinated by politics. But then, the mouse is fascinated by the snake. Or so they say."

"So what now?"

"Well, at this end, obviously, we put the arm on Claude Hubble. Meanwhile, we're also sweating Delbert Gay—who, as we already know, hired Claude Hubble. We also find out who hired Delbert."

"That could be Bruce Weston."

"Is that a hunch?" Friedman asked.

"Call it an educated guess. Weston's not telling us anything."

Sitting in Hastings's visitor's chair, elbow propped on the chair arm, chin cupped in the palm of his right hand, Friedman tapped one plump cheek with a reflective forefinger. His brown eyes were veiled. Privately, Hastings had labeled this pose Friedman's Buddha imitation.

The senior lieutenant was deep in thought, deciding strategy. Finally he spoke:

"Harold Best, I assume, lives in Los Angeles."

"Right."

"Which means," Friedman said, "that you've got to go to Los Angeles. You work from that end, try to trace the money down the ladder from Best. I'll work this end, going up the ladder from Bruce Weston. So to speak."

"I was afraid you were going to say that."

"How so?" Friedman raised his eyes to Hastings's face, searching for his meaning.

"Nobody likes working outside his own jurisdiction. Especially in Los Angeles. Christ, those guys make it up as they go along down there."

"I agree. But the alternative is to let the LAPD interrogate Harold Best, for God's sake. Which I'm sure they'd love to do. LAPD is riddled with publicity-seekers. It goes with the territory."

"If I do go down there, I should check in with LAPD, though. Protocol. And they'll want to know what I'm up to."

"So don't check in with them. What's the advantage? Except for a car, you don't need them. So you can rent a car."

"Best's got to be surrounded by people, if he's running for the Senate. Without any jurisdictional authority, I'll have a hell of a time getting through to him."

Ignoring the point, Friedman once more lapsed into deep reflection. Then, speculatively: "I'm trying to imagine how the money trail would go, from Los Angeles to San Francisco. I figure that, besides Best's father-in-law and his wife, the piranhas, there's probably two or three people who have direct access to Best. If you connected with one of them—a campaign manager, for instance—and persuaded him to hand-carry a note to Best, your troubles could be over. You know, like, 'Ah, those nights in the frat house.' Give him a place to meet you, and you'd be in business."

"You make it sound easy."

"Harold Best is carrying around a very, very big secret. He sees a note like that, he'll come running."

"Carpenter says he's really a nice guy. Very generous. Very caring."

Friedman shrugged. "He probably *is* nice. But he's weak, that's what I hear on FM radio as I'm driving to work. He lets his wife and his father-in-law pull his strings. So now, maybe he's paying the price. So pack your three-piece suit, and get a

139

shoe shine, and take your gun and cuffs and go down to LA. Rent a car. Take a few days, poke around. You could score big."

"How about if the two of us go?"

Decisively, Friedman shook his head. "Sure as hell, we get on that plane, there'd be mass murder on the steps of City Hall. Guaranteed."

"Okay." Automatically, Hastings glanced at his watch. Time: 2:45 P.M. He looked at the disarray on his desk. Saying, "Tomorrow. I'll leave tomorrow. Early."

"Good." Friedman heaved himself to his feet, and stood for a moment looking down at his co-lieutenant. Friedman had saved the hardest part for last:

"You should take someone with you."

Hastings made no reply.

"By rights, you should take the officer of record on the case."

Having remained seated while the other man spoke, Hastings decided to rise. Facing each other across the desk, they exchanged a long, probing look. Finally Hastings said, "You're talking about Janet Collier."

Friedman nodded. Saying softly: "That's true. Janet Collier. Otherwise known as Collier."

After another long moment of silent scrutiny, Hastings finally dropped his eyes, then let himself sink back into his chair. Muttering: "Goddammit." He spoke balefully.

After a backward glance, verifying that Hastings's office door was closed, Friedman also sank back into his chair. Saying: "I'm listening."

"First, I'm not going to take Janet down there—for purely personal reasons. So next in line would come Marsten, since he's the senior sergeant. Except that I don't like Marsten. Also, I wouldn't trust him on this assignment. If he saw a chance to make points for himself on a case this big, he'd do it. I won't take Canelli, I need him here, working the Hardaway case. So then I'd have to go around the squadroom. And whoever I pick, the rest of the guys would be pissed."

Friedman nodded ponderously. "I agree. But, you shouldn't go alone, without backup."

"If I were going after Claude Hubble, I'd want everything I could get. But we're talking about the so-called upper crust. Nobody's going to shoot me."

"We're talking about murder, Frank. Probably a murder that was planned in Los Angeles by people who're running scared."

"I'll be careful."

"Hmmm." Spoken doubtfully.

"Well, then," Hastings said, "you and Collier go."

In a silence that was gently playful, Friedman made no response.

"Okay, then I'll go. Alone." It was a take-it-or-leave-it offer, an ultimatum.

"Okay." Irritably Friedman spread his big, thick-fingered hands. "Fine. Good luck."

They eyed each other in a stiff, formal silence. Then, venturing a different, more conciliatory note, Friedman said, "You were telling me why you don't want to take Collier."

Hastings drew a long, deep breath. Saying: "You know damn well why I'm not taking her. You're the one who gave me the lecture. Squadroom morale, jealousy, rumors, even old-fashioned morality. Remember?"

"You're doubtless aware," Friedman countered, "that old-fashioned morality is back. Thanks in large part to AIDS."

Hastings eyed the other man, then said, "The truth is that I'd hate to walk out on Ann. And Janet won't take another woman's man. Speaking of old-fashioned morality."

141

"Since you mentioned Ann, have you told her there's some-one else?"

"I haven't told her. But I'm sure she knows. Women can feel these things."

"Men, too," Friedman observed dryly.

"Not as deeply as women."

Friedman gestured for Hastings to go on.

"The point is, I'm not ready to move out on Ann."

Friedman debated the wisdom of a wry response, then set-tled on a thoughtful, objective observation: "In all my years in this business," he said, "I've never seen a more likely prospect for command than Collier. She's smart, she's ambitious, and she's hardheaded, too. For all those reasons, she knows damn well that if you moved in with her, those sergeant's stripes would fade into the distance. Marriage, that's something else, speaking of conventional morality. But living together, other-wise known as shacking up, living in sin . . ." Friedman shook his head. "It wouldn't work. Not for Janet, anyhow."

"One big problem," Hastings said, "is Janet's kid. Her hus-band walked out on her. For years, she's raised her son—and partially supported her mother, who's also divorced."

"Does her son resent you? Is that it?"

Hastings grunted ruefully. "I've never met her son. When-ever Janet and I've met, it's been in places like the Chinese restaurant, and maybe once or twice on a park bench."

"My God," Friedman said, marveling, "this is an old-fashioned romance, you know that? A Bette Davis movie from the thirties, that's what we've got here."

Hastings made no reply; his expression was unreadable. Friedman studied him, then ventured: "Speaking of divorce and children, Ann has—what—two sons, right?"

Hastings sighed, dropped his eyes. Saying softly: "Right."

"Teenagers."

Hastings nodded.

"And they, I imagine, approve of you living with them."

"How do I answer that?"

"You don't have to answer. Remember when you and Ann came over for dinner a couple of months ago, with the Harrises and my eccentric cousin from Sandusky? And remember how Ann volunteered to help Clara with the cooking? Well, naturally, they talked while they worked, as girls will. And eventually they got around to how incredibly handsome you looked on TV the week before, whenever. So during the conversation, Ann volunteered that her two kids thought you were wonderful, or words to that effect."

Hastings snorted. "You really are an incorrigible gossip, you know that?"

"This isn't gossip," Friedman answered loftily. "This is sociology—life in America. Or, rather, divorce in America. I mean, just look at it: We've got you living here in San Francisco, where you were born, later to become a star halfback at Stanford. And we've got—"

Resigned to his fate, Hastings muttered, "Fullback."

"Whatever. Anyhow, here you are. And there's your ex-wife, the Detroit socialite, who's married to the golf pro and who's raising your teenage children in the lap of luxury in Michigan."

"Tennis pro. If you're going to hang out my dirty linen, you may as well—"

"Tennis pro. Sorry. Anyhow, you're sending your wealthy ex-wife child support, so your kids won't think badly of you. Meanwhile, Ann, the world's nicest fourth-grade teacher, is getting monthly checks from her ex-husband, the society psychiatrist who specializes in the problems of rich divor-cées—and who drives a Porsche which you, in a fit of temper, stove in with your bare hands when you pulled the driver's door off its hinges and—"

"Jesus, how long is this going on?"

"Actually, I'm finished. Except to point out what you already know: that you can't afford to get married because of all the support payments your ex-wife's lawyer loaded on you. Not to mention Ann, who would lose her alimony if—"

"*Jesus. Enough.* I've got the picture." Hastings picked up one of the Hardaway file folders, brandishing it. "Let's get down to business, and—"

"It's nothing personal. I'm just commenting on the state of marriage in America, like I said. I'm just—"

"And I'm commenting on the state of the Hardaway inves-tigation, which we've probably got at least two breaks on in the last couple of hours. And my comment is that—"

"I know what your comment is," Friedman said. "And, of course, you're right. So?" He extended his hands, palms up, an invitation.

"So, tomorrow morning, I'll leave for Los Angeles. I won't contact the LAPD. I'll rent a car, and do the whole thing my-self. I'll try to contact Harold Best. I'll lay the name on him: Randy Carpenter, that's the hook. If it works, I figure all I'll do is sit back and watch."

Friedman nodded decisively. "Good. Lay the name on him." Friedman's second nod was reflective as he said, "It's possible, of course, that Best doesn't know Hardaway is dead. Improba-ble, I admit, but still possible. Which means that you might be able to surprise him, get him talking. Meanwhile"—Friedman rose, loosened his tie, brushed from his vest the ashes from his lunchtime cigar—"meanwhile, on the home front, we'll be in hot pursuit of Claude Hubble. Also"—Friedman glanced at his watch—"also, in ten minutes, I intend to terrorize Delbert Gay."

"Remember, I've got a deal with Delbert. I don't want you to—"

"Just kidding." Friedman flipped a farewell hand, saying cheerfully: "Good luck in LA. Keep in touch." He turned, left the office. His stride was light and bouncy. This, Hastings knew, was Friedman's favorite part.

26

"There." Delbert Gay pointed across the street. "That ribs place, there. Rusty's. That's where Hubble spends a lot of time. He used to be a busboy at Rusty's. So now that he thinks he's a player, big time, he likes to hang around and show off his car and his threads."

Friedman consulted the looseleaf binder he held open on his lap. Beneath the three-way pictures of Claude Hubble, below the statistics and the family information and the known associates and the list of priors, the line labeled "Car" was blank.

"What kind of a car?" As Friedman asked the question, he passed the ID binder to Collier in the front seat. She took the kit and turned to share it with Canelli, who sat behind the wheel of the unmarked cruiser. With Friedman aboard, the motor pool had provided their best: a five-year-old Buick, fine-tuned, with top-of-the-line communications and electronics, most of which were in working condition. The Buick was parked on Divisadero, in front of a building that had once been a neighborhood movie house. On the badly abused marquee, letters clinging to a gap-toothed white plastic facade proclaimed, JESUS WILL RISE. At four o'clock on a warm afternoon in May, the sidewalks were populated by blacks of all ages and persuasions, some hostile, some watchful, some still hopeful. Before the Buick's engine had been switched off, the word had gone out: *The man* had arrived on Divisadero Street.

"Good-looking guy," Canelli commented as he studied the pictures of Claude Hubble.

"Listen," Gay complained, "I don't feel too good about this, sitting here like this. I mean, I'm known down here. The word gets out you guys're looking for Claude, and he knows I'm with you, then I've had it."

Seated beside Gay in the Buick's rear seat, Friedman eyed the other man. Then, speculatively: "Maybe I should cuff you. What d'you think?"

"Aw . . ." Gay shook his head vehemently, slouched down deeper in the seat.

"What kind of a car is Hubble driving?"

Gay shrugged. "He turns them over pretty fast. But they're always the same, Claude's cars. Big, old, usually all dented up. You know—road warrior, like that."

"So he's into cars," Canelli said. "Is that it?"

Aggrieved, Gay protested: "Hell, I don't know *what* he's into. All I know is, the longer we're here, the longer—"

"What about a girlfriend?" Collier asked as she twisted to face Gay.

"Jesus, I'm *telling* you, I don't know anything about the guy, not really. I mean, I got a couple of telephone numbers for him and that's it. I need something done, I call him. Maybe I leave a message. Anyhow, we meet somewhere, and I pay him half up front, that's usually how it goes. And then—"

"When you hired Hubble to take Charles Hardaway out," Friedman asked, "what'd you tell him? What were the instructions?"

"Jesus, Lieutenant," Gay said plaintively, "I already *told* you guys, I said for Hubble to just work the guy over. That's all, just hit him a few times, then split."

"Was he supposed to say anything to the victim?" Collier asked. "Like, 'This is from Bruce Weston,' something like that?"

"Naw, nothing like that. I mean, that's asking for trouble, something like that. All he was supposed to do was take a couple of shots, then split. Like I said."

"What about the instructions you got from Bruce Weston?" Friedman asked.

"Just what I told you before. I was supposed to check Charles Hardaway out, find out where he lives, what he did, what his schedule was. I took a couple of weeks, off and on. Then I got hold of Claude, gave him the plan."

"How long did it take Hubble after that?" Canelli asked.

"It didn't take any time at all. I had a picture of Hardaway, a telephoto shot I took. I gave Claude the picture, and gave him the plan. So then, Jesus, he did it that same night. I couldn't believe it."

"Did Weston tell you why he wanted Hardaway worked over?"

"No."

"You're sure?"

Impatiently, Gay nodded. "I'm sure. I mean, Hardaway

wasn't the first job I did for Weston, you know. Criminal lawyers, you take a peek inside their operation, you realize they need someone like me. And I need someone like Claude."

"I think," Friedman said, "that you know where we can find Claude Hubble." With the question, Friedman's voice dropped to a low, ominous note. The preliminaries were over.

"And if that proves to be the case," Friedman continued, "if you know where he is, but you don't tell us, then you're in trouble, Delbert. Do you understand?"

"Well, sure. But—"

"On the other hand, if Hubble should surface, and you tell us about it, then you do yourself some good."

No reply. But, deep within Delbert Gay's faded gray eyes, something shifted. During the time they'd been bargaining, Gay had sat far back in the Buick's rear seat, his left hand shielding his face. Now, pleading, he gestured with his free hand. "Listen, can't we go, drive a few blocks, at least? I—" He moistened his lips with the tip of a small pink tongue. "I think I might have an idea for you."

At a signal from Friedman, Canelli started the Buick, pulled out into traffic. In minutes, driving north on Divisadero, their surroundings changed. Behind them lay the desperation of the old ghetto. Ahead, Divisadero was rising toward the hills of Pacific Heights and some of the most desirable residential real estate in the world: majestically restored hundred-year-old Victorian mansions and town houses. Between the impoverished flatlands and the spectacular marine views from the hills of Pacific Heights, speculators were slowly acquiring the aging mansions as they fell into disrepair. The old buildings were being razed, replaced by luxury high-rises, some of them thirty stories tall. The views from the new high-rises rivaled those of the original Pacific Heights mansions.

149

"Where to?" Canelli asked.

"Just park anywhere," Friedman ordered, then turned to face Delbert Gay, who still sat with his face averted from the car's rear window. As Canelli pulled the Buick to the curb behind a Lincoln Town Car, Friedman said, "Okay, Delbert. You're safe. Talk to me."

"Yeah. Well, what I got, it's just something I picked up, nothing big. Except that—well—it's got to do with some money I gave Hubble to get out of town. It was a couple of thousand, in cash. Except that now I'm starting to hear he never did leave San Francisco. He just took the money and packed a suitcase, and then he started moving around, a night here, a night there. He's supposed to have a girlfriend out in Visitation Valley somewhere. Except that I don't know her name. Claude, he's pretty close-mouthed, you know. Pretty cool."

"The money you're talking about—the two thousand. Did that come from Weston, too?"

"It *will* come from Weston. Except that I don't have it yet."

Eyeing the other man speculatively, Friedman lapsed into a thoughtful silence before he reached into his pocket and produced a ten-dollar bill. "Here, this'll get you back to your office, Delbert. Keep in touch. Okay?"

"Yeah. Sure, Lieutenant. Thanks." Gay took the money, opened the Buick's rear door, and stepped out into the street.

"Jeez," Canelli said, following Gay with his eyes, "that guy's a real insect, you know that?"

Friedman nodded agreement. Then, in the crisp voice of command, he said, "We've got three things going, here. We've got to find Claude Hubble, that's first. Collier, I want you and someone else—" He paused, quickly calculating: of the fourteen inspectors in his command, he must select a middle-aged man, married, a straight arrow unlikely to hit on a young, desirable woman. Sigler: of the fourteen, only Sigler would do.

"Sigler," he said. "You and Sigler—I want you to look for Hubble. If I can break anyone else loose, I'll assign him, too."

"Am I in charge of the detail?" Collier asked. As she spoke, she visualized Bill Sigler's deeply lined face, the reassuring face of a veteran. During all his years in Homicide, Sigler had never taken the sergeant's exam. Like Friedman, Sigler had lost interest in climbing the advancement ladder.

"Yes," Friedman answered, making solemn eye contact. Repeating: "Yes, it's your detail. Your case. Right?"

"Yessir."

And to Canelli, Friedman said, "Joe, I want you to put some pressure on Bruce Weston, even if it's just to hang around his waiting room. Same thing for Delbert Gay—just let them know we're thinking about them. We've talked about Weston's part in all this—he paid Delbert Gay, and Gay paid Hubble to do the job with the iron pipe. But who paid Weston? Got it?"

Moving his lips and frowning, Canelli finally nodded tentatively. "Got it."

27

Barton Sobel pushed open the door from the hallway and consulted his watch as he entered the bullpen: more than twenty campaign workers at their desks, some of them phoning, some at the computers, all of them animated by the particular controlled frenzy of campaign politics. Taped to every wall, hanging from every ceiling fixture, covering the sides of every desk, the campaign posters proclaimed: BEST FOR THE SENATE, BEST FOR THE COUNTRY.

Sobel smiled, nodded to himself. The atmosphere was suitably electric: shades of Hitler's Nuremberg rallies, rank upon rank of Nazi banners, thousands of them, whipping in the wind. Goebbels had been the master of mass psychology. Never in the modern era had the few dominated the many so completely. *Sieg Heil!* the voices had roared in unison, echoing and reechoing across the Nuremberg plaza, the spectacle amplified by the swelling martial music. And, above the surging rabble of the faithful, the banners billowed: swastikas, hundreds of them.

Hitler, the manic tyrant, the beaming baby bouncer, the genius.

Stalin, brooding, psychotic, paranoid.

Churchill, the cigar-smoking cherub with the will of iron.

Roosevelt, the crippled patrician con man who dared to wear a cape, the best politician of them all.

And now there was Best.

Harold Best, the cipher. Amiable, yes. Photogenic, yes. Bright enough to remember his lines, yes.

Harold Best, age forty-seven. An aw-shucks smile that always worked, and a beautiful wife.

Harold Best, son-in-law of James Forster. James Forster, the paymaster. Neurotic, ruthless—wealthy beyond measure.

James Forster, with California in his pocket.

James Forster, eyeing Washington.

The obsequity that marked Sobel's progress across the bullpen was predictable: entry-level campaign professionals deferred to him, his two lieutenants nodded and smiled and returned to the strategies they were fashioning. Today's focus was on the logistics of a one-day swing later in the week through the southeast corner of the state. The subject was creative conservation and resource management. Meaning that Best would promise California water that Nevada and Colorado were reluctant to deliver—at present prices.

Seated at her desk beside his inner office door, his secretary was ready with the message slips generated during the hour and ten minutes he'd been in conference. Sitting on one of the two rental sofas provided for visitors, an anonymous man in his muscular mid-forties was looking at him. The stranger's manner was both patient and expectant, watching and waiting. His off-the-rack clothes matched his manner: conservative, unremarkable.

Carrying his attaché case in his left hand and taking the slips in his right hand, Sobel was gratified to see his secretary get quickly to her feet to open his office door. The secretary's name was Grace Pendergast. Just out of Stanford's M.B.A. program, Grace was the daughter of Albert Pendergast, state senator from Humboldt County. Like everyone in the inner circle of the Best campaign, Grace Pendergast was a high achiever, with an IQ to match.

"Are you eating lunch?" she asked.

He nodded, glanced at his watch. Time: almost ten thirty. He smiled appreciatively. Like all good assistants, Grace had learned to anticipate.

"How about a pasta salad from Amelio's?" he said. "And get something for yourself. On the campaign."

Mock-conspiratorially, she returned his smile. "Right."

With Grace at his side he placed his attaché case on the floor beside his desk. Then, still standing, he riffled through the message slips. Mixed with the standard slips were two business cards. One of the cards had been left by a television network VP in charge of sales.

The other card read *Lieutenant Frank Hastings, San Francisco Police Department*. There were two phone numbers on the lower right-hand corner of the card. *Co-Commander, Homicide Division* was printed in the lower left corner.

The stolid, watchful man in the visitors' area: a San Francisco homicide investigator. To confirm it, he waved the card at Grace. "That guy outside—he's a cop?"

She nodded. Her expression revealed nothing. Was she secretly enjoying his discomfort?

As if she had erred in disturbing the smoothly functioning tempo of his day, and therefore owed him an apology, he frowned at her. Saying peevishly: "Homicide? San Francisco Homicide?"

She shrugged. "He just showed up about a half hour ago, and asked to see whoever was in charge. I asked him what it concerned, but he just said he wanted to see you."

"Me? Particularly? By name?"

"No. He just said he wanted to see the person in charge."

Sobel drew a deep, irritable breath. "All right. Give it five minutes. Then send him in."

"The reason I'm here," Hastings was saying, "is that I want to talk with Harold Best." The detective spoke quietly, implacably. His eyes revealed nothing, his voice was equally noncommittal. Yet also implicit in the eyes and the voice was the particular economy of speech and body language that carried the full force of the law. Plainly, Hastings meant to prevail.

As a diversion, time to plan a reaction, Sobel glanced at his watch: ten forty-five. "Would you like some coffee? Pastries?"

The detective's smile was polite but remote. "No, thanks."

Acknowledging that the refusal signified an end to the preliminaries, Sobel nodded. He shifted his swivel chair enough to bring him in direct eye contact with the man from San Francisco.

"I'm sure you realize," Sobel began, "that Mr. Best is extremely busy. The election is only six months away. Meaning that we're in the process of finalizing everything. Itineraries, budgeting, the media, personnel decisions—by now, the first phase should be complete. Except that it isn't. So I doubt that you'll have much luck getting through to Mr. Best. In fact, I've got to tell you, it's surprising that you and I are having this little talk. Anyone else—someone off the street, without credentials . . ." Gracefully, Sobel spread his hands. Then he smiled engagingly. Both gestures were smoothly executed, all part of the political mover's bag of tricks.

"I understand," Hastings said, "that you're Mr. Best's campaign manager."

"Well—" Now the smile was self-deprecatory, boyish. In his handsome, urbane middle forties, Sobel projected an easygoing good humor. "That'd be a slight exaggeration, I'm afraid. There're three of us that call the shots in different aspects of the campaign—media, planning, financing. True, I'm the first among equals. But the real boss is Carolyn Best, the candidate's wife." As he said it, Sobel slid his gaze across Hastings's face, looking for a reaction. The absence of a reaction suggested that, yes, Hastings knew about Carolyn, about her status, her authority. And, proof positive, the detective asked, "What about James Forster?"

As if the question pleased him, as if he were encouraging a promising protégé, Sobel nodded. Observing casually: "You've been doing your homework, I see."

The detective made no reply.

"You haven't told me why you want to see Mr. Best," Sobel said.

"It's in connection with a case we're investigating. We think Mr. Best has some information we need."

"Down here, though—in Los Angeles—you've no authority."

Hastings shrugged. "I'm not here to arrest anyone. I'm here

to ask Mr. Best a few questions. A half hour of his time, that's all I need."

"That's all very well, but the plain truth is that I simply don't have the authority to put you in direct touch with Mr. Best."

"I think you do."

"Listen, Lieutenant." Sobel leaned into the desk, a confrontational move. Now there was no light of good-fellowship in Sobel's manner as he said, "At one level, of course, you're right. If I wanted to put you in touch with Harold Best, I could do it. However, to be perfectly candid, should I do it, my judgment would be called into question. Meaning that, at the next staff meeting, I could find myself taking orders, not giving them."

For a moment the detective said nothing, simply sitting quietly, his gaze reflective. Then, decisively, he suddenly nodded. "Okay. Then I'll talk to Carolyn Best."

"Jesus." Sobel's voice rose a plaintive half note, incredulous. "I just got through telling you, Carolyn is busier than the candidate. She—"

"Either you put me in touch with her," Hastings said, "or I'll have to find her on my own. Which means that, first, I contact the LAPD, which I haven't done so far. I'll have to tell them why I'm here. Everything. I'll give them names and places, things I have no intention of telling you. After I've done that I'll request assistance locating Mrs. Best. And, while I'm at it, I'll put in a request for Mr. Forster's address. Then I'll—"

"*Hey*," Sobel interrupted, his manner outraged. "Hey, what the hell do you think you're—"

"We might not have their private phone numbers, only the addresses. So we'll have to do the job in person. I'll ask for a couple of black-and-white cars, which is standard procedure. And, of course, there'll be a couple of unmarked cars. We'll drive up to the Best residence, and we'll demand entrance. We'll—"

"You're either bluffing, or you're insane. Do you have any idea how much power these people have?"

"The question is," Hastings countered, "do they know how much power I have?"

Sobel's only response was a contemptuous snort. Hastings, in his turn, rose to his feet. He pointed to his business card, lying on Sobel's desk.

"I've written my hotel and room number on the back. If you decide to cooperate, get me an appointment with Mrs. Best, you can call me. Otherwise"—Hastings consulted his watch—"otherwise, at one o'clock, I'll be on my way to downtown police headquarters. Meaning that, by tomorrow at this time, Mrs. Best is going to wonder what ever happened to her privacy." He went to the office door, opened it, and left the office without looking back.

28

"A case they're investigating?" Carolyn Best repeated. "That's all he said?" Carrying a portable phone, she rose from her desk, strode out to the deck. She was a tall, slim woman; she moved restlessly, purposefully. Her gestures revealed a tight, controlled anger. Once more, Barton Sobel had displeased her.

Standing at the railing of the deck, she looked out across the rooftops of Beverly Hills. Today, with light winds, an early summer smog layer covered the entire Los Angeles Basin. Still carrying the phone, she returned to her study, slid the glass door closed, turned her back on the low-lying haze.

"This Lieutenant Hastings," she said. "Tell me about him."

After a moment's thought, Sobel said, "He knows what he

wants, and he knows how to get it. I'd say he's very good at his job."

"Describe him."

"About forty-five. Speaks like he's been to college. Big, muscular—a good-looking man. Not brilliant, but certainly smart enough to get the job done. Thinks before he talks, I'd say."

"Did he ask to see me? Or Harold?"

"He wanted to see Harold, originally."

"But now he wants to see me."

"Or so he says."

"Did you tell him about me—about my function in the campaign?"

"I didn't have to tell him. He knew."

"But you don't know, really, why Hastings wants to see Harold. Just that it's in connection with a case Hastings is working on." As she spoke, she consulted her appointment calendar, glanced at her watch. Saying: "I don't want him to think he can jerk us around. But I sure as hell don't want a driveway full of police cars."

Sobel made no response.

"Where's Harold, right this minute?"

"He's in San Diego, speaking at a Rotary lunch. Then there's the Orchid Society, and the dedication of a new airport baggage-handling system. Then the Cub Scouts, an awards ceremony. He'll skip dinner, should be back here about eight o'clock."

"What about tomorrow?"

"Nothing special," Sobel answered. "We've got a planning session at one o'clock. We've got to be thinking about a swing through northern California. Including . . ." Sobel let a significant beat pass. "Including San Francisco."

"San Francisco . . ." Savoring the irony, she smiled. Then,

decisively: "It's almost noon. I want you to call Hastings at his hotel. Tell him I'll be able to see him about two o'clock."

"Really?" In the question, she could hear doubt, a challenge. Always, Sobel was pushing, questioning her decisions, her judgment.

"I'm not going to avoid this guy. That'll only make matters worse. As far as he's concerned, we've got nothing to hide."

"Okay," Sobel said doubtfully. "Whatever you say."

"Two o'clock. Here. Just Hastings. Nobody else, or there's no deal."

"Right." Still transparently doubtful.

"Thank you, Barton." She broke the connection, sat for a long moment at her desk, staring intently at the phone. Then she made the only possible decision. She lifted the phone, pressed a single button, heard the familiar voice:

"Yes?"

"There's a San Francisco detective in town. I'm seeing him at two o'clock."

"Where's Harold?"

"San Diego. He's due back in Los Angeles about eight tonight."

"Let's plan on a light dinner, here. Five o'clock, I think."

"Five. Yes."

29

Reflexively, Hastings palmed his shield as he approached the tall, elegantly paneled entry door. But here, now, in Beverly Hills, the badge meant nothing, had no authority, therefore no shock value. As he was pocketing the badge, the imposing black lacquered door swung open to reveal a tall man in his late twenties. Everything about the man suggested Ivy League: the blue blazer, gray flannel slacks, untasseled black loafers, white button-down shirt, old school tie. The man's finely drawn features were aristocratic, his dark hair was razor-cut.

"Lieutenant Hastings?" The smile was urbane, tainted by a slight suggestion of disdain. In this young man's world, policemen were members of the servant class.

"That's right. I've got an appointment with Mrs. Best."

"Yes." The urbane smile widened almost imperceptibly; the young man stepped back, gestured Hastings inside. They crossed a marble entry hall, entered a corridor that led to a suite of rooms at the rear of the Best mansion. At the end of the hallway the young man knocked discreetly on a closed door, then pushed the door open.

It was an elegantly appointed room, dominated by a huge antique claw-footed table that served as a desk. To one side were another period table and six chairs, presumably for conferences. The wall behind the desk was dominated by electronic components, computer screens, and three televisions. Sliding glass doors led to an adjoining deck. Carolyn Best stood in the open doorway to the deck. She was a tall woman, a commanding presence perfectly suited to her dramatically opulent surroundings. Her features were decisive, her shoulder-length ash-blond hair casually styled. She wore beige slacks and a tangerine silk blouse. A pair of tortoiseshell reading glasses was suspended around her neck by a golden ribbon that complemented her hair.

"Lieutenant Hastings." She gestured to a chair placed before the desk. "Sit down. Please." It was a command, not an invitation.

"Thank you."

Assuming her position behind the desk, she allowed a moment of silence to pass as she assessed her antagonist. Then abruptly she said, "What is it, exactly, that I can do for you, Lieutenant?"

"You can arrange for me to talk to your husband."

Her perfectly drawn lips stirred in a distant smile. Her eyes were a deep, startling violet. "I'm afraid," she said, "that my husband's time is oversubscribed. But if I can help you . . ." She gestured with her left hand, a graceful invitation. She wore

163

thin gold bracelets and a simple wedding band. Her eyes were shrewd, sharp-focused on her visitor.

"Sorry," Hastings countered. "But I've got to speak with Mr. Best. It shouldn't take long. A half hour, no more."

"In campaign time, Lieutenant Hastings—political time, if you will—a half hour can equal a whole day of regular time."

"Then I'll try to be brief, when Mr. Best and I talk."

Surrendering to exasperation, she sighed sharply, saying, "My husband and I operate as a team, Lieutenant. To be perfectly honest, unless you're more forthcoming, I really can't justify making time in Harold's schedule for you to see him."

Hastings studied the woman for a long, thoughtful moment before he began to speak in a quiet, measured voice:

"I can understand how you think your husband can't spare the time. I know he's a very important man. But when you talk about politics, you're talking about—" He hesitated, searching for the phrase. "You're talking about people—how they live, how they die. You're in the business of promising people a good life, making things better for them. But when things go wrong, that's my department. Someone dies, we get the call. And if it's murder, then someone has to pay. Crime and punishment, in other words. Good and evil."

"All of which," Carolyn Best said, "doesn't tell me why you're here."

"I'm conducting a murder investigation. Last Tuesday, in San Francisco, a man was murdered. Charles Hardaway. We believe your husband might be able to provide us with a motive for that murder. Or, at the least, give us some information about the victim. So I'm looking for information. Possibly vital information in an ongoing murder investigation."

"What possible connection could my husband have?"

"I'll have to discuss that with Mr. Best."

164

Anger flashed in the violet eyes. "You still don't understand, Lieutenant. My husband and I are"—impatiently, she threw out her hand—"we're synonymous. Talking to me is the same as talking to him. There's no difference."

"No difference to you, maybe. But to me, there's a big difference. Call it protocol—legally, the chain of evidence. Break the chain, and the whole case comes apart."

"But—"

"Some of the information we're looking for goes back almost thirty years, Mrs. Best. Long before you even knew your husband."

"Lieutenant . . ." Making no effort to conceal her exasperation, she drew a deep breath. The mannerism lifted her breasts. Appreciatively, Hastings conceded that Carolyn Best was an exciting, desirable woman. What would her reaction have been, discovering that her husband was bisexual? Or did she know? Was it possible that—?

"I hate to indulge in clichés," she said, her voice hard and purposeful, "but the bottom line is that my husband and I—and especially my father, James Forster—wield considerable power in this state. And the truth is, a couple of phone calls to San Francisco, and I can assure you that you'd start to have a whole hell of a lot of career problems. Instantly. 'Pounding a beat,' isn't that the phrase?"

Without fully realizing that he meant to do it, Hastings had risen to his feet. He stood for a moment looking down at Carolyn Best. Then he said, "I've been threatened many times, Mrs. Best. It worried me the first few times it happened. But I finally realized that people who make threats are frightened people. And frightened people make mistakes." Mockingly, he smiled. "Don't bother to show me out. I'll find the way."

165

30

"Where's my wife?" Best asked.

"At home, as far as I know. Actually, I haven't talked to her since that goddam detective arrived on the scene."

"Homicide, you say. San Francisco Homicide."

Sobel nodded. "Right."

They were traveling north on the Santa Monica Freeway, en route from LAX to Beverly Hills. Sobel gestured to the tiny bar built into the Lincoln's divider. "Do you mind? It's been a long day."

"Please." Best gestured to the bar. "Help yourself."

"How about you?"

"Brandy. Straight up, please."

"So—" Sobel gestured with his glass, a salute. "So how'd it go in San Diego?"

Best's smile twisted ironically. "Don't schedule me any Cub Scout functions for a while, Bart. I don't think that's where the votes are."

"Maybe not the votes. But how about photo ops?"

"Photo ops, sure. I judged a guinea pig personality contest."

"Ah, yes." Sobel nodded complacently. "Yes, I remember scheduling that personally. How'd it go?"

"Truthfully," Best admitted, "I think it came off. The advance work was good, and the turnout was great. Except that one of the contestants shit on my shoe."

Smiling, Sobel sipped his drink. "Bummer." Then, all business: "Word is, Ryder's calling it dead even in the *Sentinel* tomorrow."

"Ah." Best nodded. "That's wonderful, yes."

"The momentum—it's starting to happen, Harry."

Wearily, affably, Best smiled. "Bring on the guinea pigs, eh?"

"Exactly."

The Lincoln was turning onto Rodeo Drive; only a mile from home. Best glanced at the clock: almost nine thirty. He would have a light meal, watch the local news, get to bed early. If he missed Carolyn tonight, he would catch her tomorrow at breakfast.

"What's scheduled for tomorrow?" Best asked.

"Ten o'clock, we're roughing out the Humboldt County swing for next month. We don't need your input yet, though. There's still a lot of preliminary stuff. Those goddam old-growth redwoods, logging, the spotted owl. It's a potential minefield, everybody loses, nobody wins. So it's better if we start slowly, feel our way. Initially, I don't want you up front, not even in the meetings, the planning sessions. You'll come in late, as the all-seeing peacemaker. That's the way I see it."

"Maybe we should pass altogether."

Ruefully, Sobel shook his head. "No such luck. This one we can't pass on. No way."

"Hmmm."

The limo was slowing for the final turn into the driveway of the Best mansion. The driver's voice came over the intercom: "Shall I put the car away?"

"No," Best answered. "You'll take Mr. Sobel home. He doesn't have a car here."

"Yes, sir."

They were stopped at the gates, which were about to open. A strange car was parked close beside the gate. The car was a cheap American sedan. Moving slowly, deliberately, a man was getting out of the car on the driver's side. In the Lincoln's front seat, a case containing a MAC-10 machine pistol always rode beside the driver. As the wrought-iron gates swung slowly inward, the driver reached for the case. In the headlight glare, the stranger was raising both arms, palms outward, a gesture of peace. Something metallic sparkled in the stranger's hand. Now the gates were almost fully open. But the stranger stood in the driveway, blocking them. As Best muttered an obscenity, Sobel said, "That's him. The detective from San Francisco. Hastings."

There was a moment of silence. In the front seat, the driver was opening the small case that held the gun.

"No," Best said. "Not the gun. Close the case." And to Sobel, Best snapped, "Leonard'll take you home, then he'll come back. I'll see you at the staff meeting tomorrow—the military base closures, cutbacks in defense."

"But don't you want me to take care of this cop, send him on his way? I mean, Christ, we don't need him prowling around, harassing you."

"The best thing is to talk to him, defuse him, send him back to San Francisco." In the headlights, the figure was lowering his arm, steadily advancing on them.

"Whatever you say." Grudgingly, Sobel tripped the door latch, got out of the Lincoln's backseat, got in the front with the driver. Equality in the ranks, after all, was a hallmark of the Best campaign.

Best was smiling a campaign smile as he got out of the limo and advanced to meet the man from San Francisco.

"We've been talking for twenty minutes, Mr. Best. And the truth is, I don't think we're connecting. It's like you're talking at one level, and I'm talking at another level. And nothing's happening."

"I'm sorry you feel that way, Lieutenant. Because I'm trying to help you. But you've got to realize that I'm running for United States senator from California, which has a bigger economy than most countries of the world. And if you follow politics, you realize that the slightest hint of scandal, so-called, even if it's in the past, is the end of everything."

"Which is why," Hastings said, "you won't admit to knowing Randall Carpenter in college. Is that what you're saying?"

They were in a small den just off the main entry hall of the Best mansion. Holding a stem glass half-filled with seltzer water, Best stood behind his leather-topped desk. He was a tall, athletic man, almost improbably handsome. Was it possible, Hastings wondered, that a subspecies of the American male

169

was emerging: the tawny blond, bronzed, blue-eyed Californian who smiled so easily, played tennis so gracefully, pleased so many, and offended so few?

The time was after ten o'clock. Seated in a brass-studded leather visitor's chair, Hastings decided to remain silent as he tracked the other man with his eyes. Because he'd been thirsty, Hastings's own glass of seltzer water was empty and rested now on the desk, pointedly ignored by his host.

Finally, sighing with sharp impatience, Best decided to sit behind his desk. For the first time he spoke harshly, a hint of the supercilious man behind the smile:

"I believe," Best said, "that the term is *shakedown*. Could that be it, Lieutenant? Could it be that you ran across someone called Carpenter, who claimed that he knew me in college? And could it be, further, that Carpenter alleges that he and I had some kind of a sexual relationship? And could it therefore be that, having discovered this little nugget, you decided to take a few days off from the SFPD? Could that account for your presence here? Is it possible that you decided to offer me a deal? A pledge not to reveal this alleged affair in exchange for—well, you fill in the blank. As in blank check. Is that what we're talking about here?"

Furious, holding himself painfully in check, Hastings spoke in a low, tight voice: "No, Mr. Best, that's not it. And to prove it, let's forget about what happened to you in college. Let's forget about Randall Carpenter. Okay?"

Best sipped his seltzer water as he stared at the other man. Then, softly, inscrutably, Best said, "You've got the floor, Lieutenant. Make your point."

"My point is, I'm not here to shake you down. I'm here be-

170

cause I'm investigating the murder last Tuesday night of one Charles Hardaway."

No response. Nothing but Best's improbably blue eyes, utterly empty of expression, fixed on Hastings.

"Did you know Charles Hardaway, Mr. Best?"

The reply came quickly, assertively, smoothly: "No, sir. Sorry."

"Have you ever heard of the name?"

"No, sir, not to my knowledge. I might've heard the name in passing, but it didn't register."

"Mr. Hardaway and Mr. Carpenter lived together in San Francisco until Mr. Hardaway's death, last Tuesday. They were lovers."

The other man's eyes remained utterly empty, inscrutable.

"You still maintain that you didn't know Charles Hardaway?"

"Sorry, Lieutenant. But to the very best of my knowledge I've never heard the name. *Never.*"

"Mr. Sobel—is it possible that he was in contact with Hardaway during the past several months? Without your knowledge?"

Best raised his shoulders in an ironic shrug. "You'd have to ask Mr. Sobel. Wouldn't you?"

"Let's get back to shakedowns, Mr. Best, since you introduced the subject. Okay?"

No reaction. No hint of even the slightest misgiving was visible in the other man's face. Best's long, graceful fingers, toying with the stem glass, were perfectly steady.

"I have testimony that, when Mr. Carpenter contracted AIDS, and could no longer work, he went to you with a request for money. Is that true?"

Harold Best calmly studied his antagonist. Finally Best said, "Let's assume that's true. How could it bear on the murder of Charles Hardaway?"

"Because when Hardaway saw how easy it was to get money from you, he decided to go into business for himself. He contacted you and put the arm on you. It worked—at least for a few months. We're close to reconstructing a paper trail that connects you to Hardaway, and it involves several cash transactions. But then Hardaway apparently got greedy, which is the mistake blackmailers usually make. He threatened you with exposure, because he knew of your relationship with Carpenter. So you didn't have a choice. You ordered Hardaway attacked. You told an underling, who contacted his people in San Francisco. They hired a professional to do the job. And he was very good at what he did. He—"

"Jesus." Best suddenly exploded, rising to his full height behind the desk, sending his chair crashing into the wall. Fists clenched, voice raised furiously, he began to sputter incoherently for a moment. Then: "Jesus, you—you're fantasizing, you dumb son of a bitch. You—you're out of control. I'd advise you to get back in your car, and drive to the airport, and catch the first flight back to San Francisco. And when you get back to San Francisco, I'd advise you to keep a very goddam low profile. I'd also advise you to stay away from Randy. Stay away from this whole thing. Because if you don't, I promise you'll pay. You'll pay and pay and pay."

"I notice," Hastings said, speaking quietly, complacently, "that you said 'Randy.' Are you aware that you did that—said 'Randy' in a very familiar voice? Because, during this whole interview"—as he spoke, Hastings unbuttoned his shirt to reveal a tiny microphone clipped to the V-neck of his T-shirt—

"during this whole interview, I made it a point to say either 'Mr. Carpenter,' or else 'Randall Carpenter.' But never 'Randy.'"

Voice quivering, Best pointed to the door. "Get out. Now. Right now. Before I call my lawyer."

Moving with great deliberateness, Hastings nodded politely to the other man, then left the room.

31

The twenty minutes following the detective's departure had given him time to plan, to rehearse his lines. Whenever it was necessary to confront her, success was possible only with an airtight script, a beginning, a middle, and an end. Plus a hook— one succinct phrase that would put her on the defensive. Then, when she was off balance, it was possible to—

A buzzer sounded: the front door. He switched on the TV monitor, focused on the foyer. The time registered on the screen: exactly 10:30 P.M. Now Carlos came into the frame. The houseman's tie was loosened and he wore slippers, an after-ten dispensation from the rules of the house. Carlos opened the front door as he half-bowed to Carolyn, who was smiling generously, a sprightly pantomime. Carolyn and Carlos had always understood each other.

She had advanced midway into the central hallway when Best opened the den door and stepped out to greet her. He was conscious of the moment's tableau: she so stylish, so completely in command, placing her attaché case on a side table, tossing back her thick tawny hair, glancing casually at presorted pieces of the day's mail that had been put in a Chinese bowl in the foyer. He decided not to advance on her. Instead, he chose to stand before the open doorway to his den, his one true refuge. Here, now, she must come to him.

He watched her slit one envelope open, glance at the one-page letter inside. She smiled faintly. Whatever the letter concerned, she'd correctly guessed its contents, and had already discounted them. She returned the mail to the bowl, to be dealt with tomorrow. Then she turned to face him.

"So . . ." She smiled: a predictably impersonal smile that was nevertheless friendly, perpetually amused. The smile, he knew, had been created over the years especially for him. The casual contempt at the secret center of the smile was visible only to him.

"So how was San Diego?" She had advanced to stand almost within arm's length, a carefully calculated distance. Perhaps because she sensed that the San Diego swing might have misfired, the smile widened almost imperceptibly, yet tolerantly. Between them, his failure was common currency.

It required that he respond in kind: "A guinea pig shit on my shoe during the Boy Scout thing."

"Cub Scout," she corrected automatically.

"Cub Scout." As he spoke, he stepped aside, gesturing her into his den. "Got a minute?"

She glanced at her watch, shrugged, preceded him into the den. Best closed the door, took his accustomed place behind the desk. Carolyn sat facing him across the desk, her accustomed place.

"Were you at your father's?" It was a carefully calculated opening gambit.

Studying his face, she nodded. He'd gotten her attention; he could see it in her eyes, in the stillness, the covert watchfulness.

"It's Hastings," he said. "The policeman from San Francisco. You saw him today. Didn't you?"

Still watching him carefully, she said nothing.

"You saw Hastings," he repeated. "I know you saw him."

"All right, Harry, I saw him." She spoke coolly, calmly. Then, glancing at her watch, she sighed. Carolyn never voluntarily stayed up after eleven o'clock.

"And then," he pressed, "you went to see your father. You drove yourself—in the Buick."

The last phrase amused her. "Implying," she said, "that it was all very hush-hush."

"Just James and you. All the servants out of the house. Am I right?"

With seeming indifference, she shrugged. Then: "Whatever it is, Harry, make it short, will you? We've got a busy day tomorrow."

"Aren't you curious about Lieutenant Hastings, Carolyn? I talked to him, too, you know. Aren't you curious?"

This time, her sigh was impatient as she glanced at her watch. The message: his time was running out.

Aware of the enormous weight of the words he'd rehearsed so remorselessly during the past twenty minutes, he spoke softly, sibilantly: *"Charles Hardaway."* He let a beat pass, focusing her attention. "You and Hastings talked about Charles Hardaway." Another short, probing silence. "You talked about Charles Hardaway and I talked about his lover, Randy Carpenter."

Seated in one of the small room's two wine-colored leather armchairs, she remained motionless, her violet eyes revealing nothing as she stared at him across the desk. Yet behind her facade, he could sense the gathering tension, the latent fury.

"You're wrong," she said. "He mentioned Hardaway's name, but wouldn't tell me anything."

"I told you about Randy," he said. "In college, we—"

"I know," she snapped. "I know. And I told you, Harold, that you'd been a fool."

He waved away the criticism. "Randy isn't the problem, Carolyn, and never was. The problem is Charles Hardaway. Alive or dead. And Hardaway is your problem. Not my problem. Your problem. Especially now—especially dead."

"My problem?" The contempt behind the words was palpable. "*My* problem? How do you figure that, Harry?" Now she spoke bitterly, as if she'd been betrayed.

"The only plausible scenario here is that Hardaway found out about Randy and me. Somehow he got through to you—or your father."

"That's supposition, Harry. Speculation. You're assuming that—"

"Who else could it be, Carolyn? He must have tried to blackmail me and you stepped in. Who else would pay? It was blackmail, and you paid. And paid. Until you realized you had to have him killed. So your father must have arranged it, no problem. I can imagine how it went. There're a dozen people in San Francisco who'd do anything—*anything*—to ingratiate themselves to your father. All he had to do was give one of them

Hardaway's name. And that was it." He spread his hands. "Hardaway died. End of the problem. Washington, here we come."

Her response was a small, reflective smile that was palpably edged with both pity and derision. "God, you're such a child, Harry. I wish I had the luxury of appreciating your innocence. You're—"

"You two must have had Charles Hardaway killed, Carolyn. And the police are going to find out about it. Murder. My God, we could all be—"

"It wasn't murder. Not premeditated murder. It was a warning—a beating. Something went wrong, that's true. But it was never murder."

"Hardaway's dead. That's murder."

For a moment she said nothing, did nothing but sit silently, her eyes locked with his. Finally she spoke: "If you and Randy Carpenter hadn't played around in college, none of this would be happening. You're the problem. When you and Randy—"

"All Randy did was ask for money. He's got AIDS, and he's desperate. And all I did was send him money periodically."

"Blackmail. *You* paid blackmail."

"No. If those payments stopped, he'd never threaten me. He'd never talk. Never."

"Bullshit."

For a long, harsh moment they said nothing. Until, speaking calmly and concisely, Best said, "The police aren't going to let go of this. They've got a murder, and they've got a motive, which was to shut up Hardaway. This detective—Hastings—he's only the first. There'll be others poking around. And eventually they'll find whoever killed Hardaway. They'll find out why, too. And that'll be the end of the campaign. The media—God—it'll be a feeding frenzy." He permitted himself a small smile. "Your father must've been furious, when it all hit the fan."

"If he's furious with anyone, it's you, Harry. My God, all you had to do was keep your place in the script." She shook her head slowly in disgust.

"Randy came to me, and I handled it, no problem. But when Hardaway came to you—Sobel, whoever—you fucked up. 'Pay me,' Hardaway said, 'or I'll call the media.' And you paid. Then you panicked, and you had him killed. So now we'll have the media *and* the police. We're screwed."

"We're *not* screwed. My God, one detective with run-over shoes rings your bell, and you panic."

"I think *you're* panicking, Carolyn. In your own quiet, over-privileged way, you're losing it."

"How much money do you send Carpenter?"

"About five or six thousand a month."

"But in a few months he'll be dead. Right?"

Resigned, he nodded.

"So there's no problem, with Randy. He's no blackmailer, you say. And he's dying." She spoke more concisely now. As always, the elements of her calculations were clicking efficiently into alignment.

"That still leaves Hardaway."

"No." Gently, she shook her head. Repeating softly, with malicious precision: "No. That leaves Hardaway's murderer."

"The murderer your father hired."

"Oh, no, Harry." She spoke mockingly, superciliously amused. "The murderer was hired by some nameless flunky in San Francisco. Who, in turn, was hired by another nameless flunky, probably a lawyer. Who, in turn, was retained by someone else. A system of cutouts, in other words. You know how it goes."

179

"I know about cutouts. And I know about people paying off other people in cash for shady services rendered. But murder . . ." Despairingly, he shook his head. Suddenly he realized that he'd lost the edge of anger that had taken him this far. Now fear was engulfing him, stifling him. Two hours ago, he had been secure in his limo, drinking brandy with Sobel, tie loosened, exchanging quips; his world had been secure on its axis—good-bye California, hello Washington.

But then a figure had materialized in the darkness beside the entrance to the estate. A detective. Lieutenant Frank Hastings, badge in hand, the stalker, dressed in a suit that didn't quite fit. Fate, the stalker, the avenger. Meaning that now, even in the security of his den, his world was tilting, falling away, leaving him limp with fear, once more a victim to the ravages of Carolyn's scorn. Carolyn and her father. They would always circumscribe his life, hold him helpless. For twenty minutes, after Hastings had left and before Carolyn arrived, he had believed he could bend them to his power, the power of fear for the omnipotence of the law. He'd been wrong. Nothing, not even murder, could loosen their hold on him.

Dominant again, she rose and stood for a moment looking down at him as he sat behind his elegant antique desk. Never, he realized, had Carolyn looked so completely in command.

"Don't worry about Randy," she said, speaking calmly. "Pay him, be nice to him, make him feel secure—and let him die."

Somehow unable to stand and face her, he could only remain seated as he nodded, mumbled something unintelligible.

"You can forget about Hardaway, too, forget about his death. It'll be taken care of. The whole thing, it's being handled." Complacently, almost casually, she smiled.

32

Hastings aimed the TV wand, pressed the Off button, plunged the room into darkness. He turned to lie on his back, staring up at the ceiling.

Until now, he hadn't paused long enough to reflect on the day. Barton Sobel, Carolyn Best, and Harold Best—three targets of opportunity all in a row, plink, plink, plink, with none of the problems usually encountered getting through to the rich and the famous.

Why?

Why had Carolyn Best and her husband made it so easy?

Because, probably, they hoped to discover how much he knew—and didn't know.

Carolyn, the piranha.

Harold Best, the figurehead, the front man who mouthed his lines according to whatever script his wife and her father chose for him.

Carolyn, the cagey one.

Harold, the short-fused one, the ineffectual one.

And Carolyn's father, James Forster—the elusive one.

Tomorrow, should he try to get through to James Forster? Or should he return to San Francisco and leave them wondering? If he left Los Angeles, mission apparently accomplished, would the suspects begin to suspect one another, would there be a falling-out of co-conspirators?

He yawned, turned on his side—made his decision. He would sidestep James Forster, the godfather. He would return to San Francisco tomorrow, do whatever it took to find Claude Hubble. They would offer Hubble a deal, begin climbing the chain of evidence, bottom to top: Hubble, Delbert Gay, Bruce Weston—and up and up, in San Francisco. Then, with a solid evidence chain, he would bring Friedman to Los Angeles. Friedman would assume center stage, wheeling and dealing, manipulating, trading half-promises for half-truths—all the while smiling inscrutably.

He and Friedman . . .

And Janet, too?

Janet . . .

He turned on his back, yawned, turned on his left side, yawned again.

Janet . . .

Had he insisted, she could have come to Los Angeles with him. She was, after all, the officer of record on the case. The interview with Sobel, the interrogation of Carolyn Best, then Harold Best, even conceivably an interview with James Forster—it could have been her prerogative to participate in all of it.

Incredibly, in little more than a week, beginning with a seemingly random street crime, a bashing, the case had mushroomed, and now pointed, amazingly, to the most powerful political overlords in California: Harold Best, his wife, his father-in-law.

Harold Best, soon to be the junior senator from California.

Harold Best, bisexual.

Harold Best, ostensibly so pleasant, so open-faced, so affable—and yet, certainly, so conniving, so devious.

Would Janet have been more successful with Best than he'd been? As a team, could they have learned more?

Yes, almost certainly they would have learned more. Already, he and Janet had developed a feel for interrogation, for working efficiently together. He would take the lead, laying it out, setting the tone. She would wait and watch, looking for her opportunity to insert the single question that might throw the suspect off balance, setting him up for Hastings's next thrust. Good cop, bad cop.

How would she have reacted, if he'd offered her the chance to go to Los Angeles? How would—?

On the nightstand close beside his bed, the telephone warbled. Half asleep, he lifted the receiver.

"It's not quite eleven," Friedman's voice said in his ear. "Okay?"

"Yeah." Yawning, he levered himself against the headboard to sit up. "Yeah. No problem."

"So. How'd it go?"

"Who knows? I talked to Best's campaign manager, a guy named Barton Sobel, who seems to have lots of clout. He shut me out, initially, but then I think he told Best's wife that she should see me, that's my guess. Anyhow, she did. She didn't give me a thing, but I think I shook her up. I think I shook up Harold Best, too."

"What about Forster?"

"I ran out of time. But now I'm thinking maybe it was just as well."

"How so?"

"When I got here, I decided to rent a car at the airport, try to slide into town nice and easy, see how lucky I could get, without contacting LAPD. And I *did* get lucky—very lucky, I figure. I made three solid connections with no one from LAPD looking over my shoulder. But I don't think it'll last. I figure once Carolyn Best and her husband talk to Forster, then sure as hell the LAPD's going to be all over me. So I'm thinking I should get out of town tomorrow, give Forster time to stew, go back to San Francisco and help find Claude Hubble."

"I like it," Friedman announced. "So, since I'll see you tomorrow, and since it's now eleven, I'll let you get to sleep."

"Good. See you tomorrow." Hastings cradled the phone, switched off the light, settled himself in the bed—and began thinking of Janet Collier, recalling the moment he'd first seen her: a stranger, pulled in at random as backup on an operation that had almost cost Hastings his life. Their attraction had grown over the next few months as they worked together, while their personal lives kept them apart. Two frustrated lovers, both of them trying to make sense of their lives. Meanwhile, tonight, they each slept alone.

33

"So," Friedman said, easing himself into Hastings's visitor's chair. "Tell me about Los Angeles. I was amazed that you got to Harold Best. How'd you manage it?"

"I honest to God don't know. But I think I stirred things up, which is what I wanted to do. Sobel, the campaign manager—Carolyn Best—Harold Best—I think there's a possibility they're all involved. But until we collar Claude Hubble and go to work on him, we aren't going to get anywhere in Los Angeles. It just won't happen."

"The word we're getting," Friedman said, "is that Claude Hubble is still in town, in deep cover, very difficult to turn up. Apparently Hubble is very cool, very smart. Very trendy, too, very with it. He doesn't hang around with other blacks much, likes white girls. He's a good dresser, but not loud. He's good-looking, too. He's also slippery as hell. In his early twenties he was considered a pretty fair boxer, which is how he got in the leg-breaking business. Apart from that, though, he's done a little of everything. Including six months as a security guard. He keeps moving. All of which is why it's hard to collar him."

"He's been arrested, though."

Friedman shrugged. "Shoplifting, car boosting, a little burglary. Nothing heavy."

"Without Hubble," Hastings said, "we've got nothing."

"Even with him, we've also got nothing—not compared to what there is to get. I mean, Jesus, all we'd have is little fish with Hubble and Delbert Gay. But then there's this big gap, even with Weston, until we get to the campaign and the Bests."

"I know . . ."

"Next time you go to LA," Friedman said, "I'll go with you. I'd love to see these fat cats squirm."

"Great. Let's do it."

"First, we need Hubble. Who, in fact, Canelli and Collier are working on right this minute. Last night it looked like they were just a step behind him. Collier, apparently, connected with Hubble's girlfriend, who's nineteen and white and who works in an insurance office and who's crazy about him even though she's also very nervous about shacking up with him. Her name is Joyce Trigstadt. She apparently comes from the Midwest somewhere and her parents are very heavy-duty fundamentalists. So, of course, she rebelled, and came to the big city, and ended up in bed with a black guy. So then—"

Hastings's phone rang: the dispatcher's communications circuit. He listened for a moment, then put the call on a speakerphone. It was Canelli, calling from the field:

"Ah, Lieutenant, I'm glad I got you."

"What's up, Canelli?"

"Well, it looks like we might've made contact with Hubble. Except that it looks like Collier's radio is shot, so I thought I should call you. I mean, we might have a delicate situation here."

"What's that mean?"

"Well, there's this girl named Joyce, who's got a thing going with Hubble. She's—"

"I know about her."

"Oh. Good. Well, Collier and I've been staking her out, and we got here early this morning, like about eight o'clock. So Collier decided to follow Joyce when she went to work, which is downtown, just to check out whether Joyce really had the job she said she had. So then, when everything looked normal at the subject's office, Collier came back to Joyce's apartment building, which is on Third Avenue right near Clement. We were hoping Hubble would show up, see. Which, in fact, I guess he did, when Collier was gone, and I was alone in front, leaving the rear open until Collier got back. I mean, it was one of those surveillance screwups that happen all the time, with just two people. And it looks like Hubble came in the back while I was in the front, alone. I mean, these things happen, you know?"

"I know, Canelli. So?"

"Well, maybe a half hour ago, I went to take a leak. So what happened, I guess, was that Joyce must've arrived home early from downtown, because when I was around the corner, taking my leak, I heard Collier on the surveillance radio, except that I couldn't hear what she was saying very well. I think her nicad battery was low. But obviously she was talking to a woman with her mike open, so I could hear. But, like I said, I couldn't really hear what she was saying from where I was. So I went back to the apartment building. And, Jesus, there's no one there."

Exchanging an alarmed glance with Friedman, Hastings asked, "What d'you mean, Canelli? What about Jan—what about Collier?"

"Well, jeez, the way I figure it could've happened, beginning this morning, Hubble got into the apartment building when I was in front, waiting for Collier to come back from downtown, where she was following Joyce. Maybe Hubble snuck into Joyce's apartment from the back, and went to sleep, who knows? So when Collier came back from downtown—that was about nine, nine thirty this morning—Hubble was already inside, but we didn't know it. Quite a coincidence, eh?"

"Canelli—what about Collier, for God's sake?"

"Yeah. Well, that's what I'm telling you. When I went to take a leak, Collier was watching the front, like I said. And I figure that Joyce Trigstadt came home early from work, while I was around the corner. That was about one thirty, maybe a half hour ago. I figure Collier intercepted Joyce outside her building, that much I got from Collier's surveillance radio. But then, when I got back, there was no Collier and no Joyce. So I figure Collier went up to Joyce's place, with her radio transmitting. And I figure that Hubble was there, waiting for them."

"You mean he was waiting for Collier? An ambush?"

Across the desk, Hastings saw Friedman's eyes widen with alarm. It was a worrisome sight; Friedman never let his misgivings show.

"I don't know about an ambush. All I know is that, on my radio, I could hear two women and a man talking. I couldn't make out many of the words. But, definitely, there's a man up there."

"Where're you now?"

"I'm parked in our cruiser, in front. And I've got two uniforms at the back. With radios."

"How about the roof?"

"No problem. The building isn't attached."

"How about Collier's radio? Still putting out?"

"Not for about the last fifteen minutes."

"Okay—I'll get a couple of people. What's the address?"

"Three-twenty-one Third Avenue. Near Clement."

"Okay. Keep in touch with Lieutenant Friedman. I'm on my way." Shaking his head, Hastings cradled the telephone. Saying angrily: "That's some shitty stakeout."

"These things happen," Friedman said. "You'd better get started."

34

"Is her name on the mailbox?" Hastings asked.

"Yessir," Canelli answered.

"What about Collier's radio? Anything?"

"Nothing. Not even static."

"Collier should've known better than to go into a building alone, goddammit."

"Except that she sure as hell didn't know Hubble was there. She just met Joyce out in front of the building, and decided to go up to Joyce's apartment, that's the way I got it from her radio."

"Is Collier on channel B?"

"Yessir."

"Well, let's do it." He picked up his own radio and tuned it to surveillance channel B, the operation's assigned channel. He checked the net: Sigler and two uniformed officers at the rear, concealed, he and Canelli and Marsten in front, parked in an unmarked car. All five radios came in loud and clear, both transmitting and receiving. From Collier, the sixth radio, there was only static, broken by sounds that might be voices.

"Canelli and I'll go in," Hastings said, speaking into his radio. "Marsten stays in our unit. Understood?"

Sigler and the two uniformed men acknowledged.

"Remember, there're probably three souls: Janet Collier, Claude Hubble, who's a young black male, about five-ten, one hundred fifty pounds, and Hubble's girlfriend. Collier is about a hundred twenty, dark hair in a ponytail, slim. She's wearing beige slacks and a suede jacket." He looked at Canelli for confirmation. Canelli nodded, then supplied a description of Joyce Trigstadt: young, blond, wearing a sweater and skirt, dressed for business in the financial district. "We don't know what Hubble is wearing," Hastings said.

"Be careful, Lieutenant." It was Sigler, in the rear. As always, Sigler spoke from the heart, however diffidently. Seated in the rear seat of Hastings's cruiser, Marsten said nothing. Always the resentful one, Marsten plainly believed he should be going in, not Canelli.

"Marsten, you handle communications. And you'll be in command outside the building."

Grudgingly, Marsten nodded agreement. Medals weren't awarded for backup.

The building was six stories and contained ten apartments plus a full-width garage. It was a fifties-vintage white stucco building, hand-textured and trimmed in fake Spanish colonial: red tiles bordering the flat roof, hand-hewn exterior beams that supported nothing. In the entry there were red floor tiles and white tiles on the walls. The glass door was protected by a wrought-iron grille. Obviously the building was well maintained. The bank of brass mailboxes had been recently polished. Joyce Trigstadt's apartment was number 5. No mail was visible in apartment 5's mailbox. At three o'clock on a Thursday afternoon, most of the mailboxes contained mail. Hastings glanced at Canelli; yes, Canelli had checked the mailbox. The entrance to the building was set back from the sidewalk; shrubbery grew close to the walkway that led to the lobby, offering cover from prying eyes.

"Give it a try," Hastings said as he turned his back on Canelli to face the sidewalk.

"Yessir." Canelli drew a set of lock picks from an inside pocket, stooped in front of the glass entry door, and began working the picks. The lock was old and loose, and it quickly yielded. Gratified, Canelli smiled as he pushed the door open. Like the exterior, the interior lobby was clean and orderly, with a figured rug and a mission-style Mexican table and two chairs. Mail and small packages were scattered on the table. At the far end of the lobby, a stairway with a wrought-iron railing led up to the second floor. As Hastings walked to the staircase, he clipped his surveillance radio's tiny microphone to the lapel of his jacket and fixed the transparent earpiece more firmly in his ear, saying, "Check in." Sigler, in back, and Marsten, in front, acknowledged the call loud and clear. Canelli made the final call.

Climbing the stairs, Hastings unbuttoned his tweed sport jacket and loosened his four-inch service revolver in its spring holster. Behind him, Canelli was doing the same.

Apartments 1 and 2 occupied the second floor, meaning that the entire ground floor was the building's garage. Apartments 3 and 4 would occupy the next floor. Apartment 5 would be the fourth-floor rear.

From apartment 1 came the sound of light rock. Two parcels and a folded newspaper were piled in front of apartment 2. Hastings glanced at Canelli, got a nod in return. Canelli was focused on the next floor—and then the next floor, with apartment 5. In Canelli's soft brown eyes, Hastings could see a quickening, the avidity of the chase. Once more, they exchanged nods. Then, moving silently, Hastings was ascending the stairs to the third floor. As his head came even with the floor, he looked up and down the deserted third-floor hallway. With Canelli three steps behind, Hastings began another ascent until he was standing in the fourth-floor hallway. Yes, 5 was to his right, at the rear of the building. And, yes, 6 was to his left, at the front of the building. And, yes, he saw a fire door at the rear of the corridor, across from 5. Hubble had used the fire stairs, Canelli believed, to enter the building from the rear.

As Hastings exchanged a final cautionary look with Canelli, he suddenly heard garbled, static-sizzled voices on the radio. Canelli, too, heard the fragmentary transmission: unmistakably Janet Collier's voice cutting in and out. There was another voice, too: a man, saying something indistinguishable. Then, once more, the radio went dead.

Standing side by side in the deserted fourth-floor corridor, the two men were silent, listening. Finally Hastings sighed, gestured to apartment 5's door. "What d'you think?" he whispered. "Talk our way in, or break our way in?"

Doubtfully, Canelli shook his head. "I don't know, Lieutenant. These damn doors look pretty solid. Plus, it's hard to tell what's happening. I mean, from what I heard earlier, it didn't sound like they knew Collier was a cop. It sounded like everything was cool."

"You think so?"

"Well, hell, I'm guessing. But that's the way it sounded to me. It sounded like they were—"

In Hastings's ear, the radio crackled, came to life again: most certainly Claude Hubble speaking, confirmed by the soft burr of ghetto patois: "I mean, guns're for amateurs, the way I see it. Guns're—" Once more, the radio went dead.

"Jesus," Canelli breathed. "That don't sound so good." Frowning, he eyed the door to apartment 5.

Holding the surveillance microphone close to his mouth, Hastings whispered, "We're going in. Don't acknowledge." And to Canelli he whispered, "You've got the weight."

"Yeah. Right." Canelli moved away from the wall beside the door, stepped to the opposite wall, faced the door.

"You go right," Hastings breathed. "I'll go left." Revolver ready, he took Canelli's place beside the door. One last time, they nodded. Revolver raised, Canelli lunged forward, struck the door just below the knob with his right foot. Wood splintered, the door swung sharply open, banged against an interior wall as Canelli fell flat to the right in the open doorway. Hastings leaped left, traversed the small foyer in two strides. Crouched low, shouting *"Police! Freeze!"* he trained his revolver on the trio in the room. Hubble sat on a sofa beside a young woman: Joyce Trigstadt, terrified, her whole body rigid, frozen by fear. Hubble's left hand was knotted in the woman's long, tangled blond hair. His right hand held a Buck knife against her neck, just below the ear. Beneath the knife, blood streaked the woman's neck. It was a superficial cut, not serious.

Seated in an armchair across a large, cluttered glass-topped coffee table, Janet Collier held her Glock nine-millimeter semiautomatic in both hands, the approved combat grip. The

Glock was aimed at Hubble, who was pressed close beside Joyce Trigstadt. It was a standoff.

With his revolver trained on Hubble, Hastings spoke softly over his shoulder to Canelli: "Outside, Joe. Close the door and keep it closed."

"Yessir," Canelli breathed.

"Make the calls."

"Yessir." With his own revolver trained on Hubble, Canelli began backing toward the door. When Hastings heard the door close, then heard Canelli speaking into his radio, he slowly advanced until he stood beside Janet Collier.

"How long's it been?" Hastings asked.

"About an hour," Collier answered. Her voice was steady, her eyes were hot and bold, staring at Hubble, hardly blinking. Collier was outraged. The Glock was steady as death.

Hastings turned to face Hubble. Saying: "I'm a lieutenant in Homicide, co-commander. My name is Frank Hastings. Anything you've got to say, you say it to me. I'm the man."

"Yeah . . ." Hubble was smiling, playing his ultra-tough, extra-cool role to perfection. He moved his eyes to Collier. "Yeah, she's been telling me about you, how you're the man, all right."

"We've got to talk, Claude. Let's put the weapons away. Then we'll talk." Hastings lowered his revolver until the muzzle pointed to the floor. After a moment's hesitation, Collier did the same. Both pistols remained cocked.

"I'll bet," Hubble said, "that there'll be maybe fifty cops outside. I bet they'll have the whole building covered. I bet they've got assault rifles, and helmets, and vests, the whole thing. And the TV crews, they're out there, too. All that, because of this—"
He drew back the knife a scant few inches, fondly rotating the

195

blade. The blade was bright, polished steel, flecked with fresh blood.

"Oh, Jesus," Joyce Trigstadt moaned. "Jesus, Claude. Please. Listen to what they say."

"What they're saying, Joyce, is for me to put down the knife, and let them take me off to jail. That's what they're saying."

"Claude . . ." Terrified, the woman tried to move away from her tormentor. Instantly, the knife touched her neck.

With his eyes locked into Hubble's bully-boy gaze, Hastings spoke to Janet Collier.

"How'd it get to this?"

"She came home about one thirty," Collier said. "She saw me in my car, in front of the building, and she came over. She wanted to talk upstairs. I'd talked to her last night, and I thought we could connect. I knew Canelli would be back in a few minutes, so I didn't think it was a risk. I set my radio, and came up here with her. Hubble was already in the bedroom."

"He was waiting for you. Is that it?"

Hubble answered the question: "They came through the door, Joyce first. I was in the bedroom, sleeping. But I was quick. I heard a key in the lock, I was already behind the door, waiting for it to open. I was ready."

"You played off a knife against a gun." Hastings spoke scornfully, a calculated blow to the ego. "You call that ready?"

"Yeah, well, she was pretty quick with her gun, I'll say that for her." He smiled at Collier. She nodded grim acknowledgment. Her Glock still pointed down.

"The word we have on you, Hubble," Hastings said, "is that you're smart. But this—" With his revolver, Hastings gestured in a short, mocking arc. "This is dumb. What'll this get you but more trouble?"

"Well, you want to know the truth, this whole thing

was—" Hubble frowned, searching for the word. He was slim, wiry, and quick-talking. His voice was softly burred. He was dressed only in white boxer shorts and a white T-shirt. His arms and thighs were muscle-corded. He wore his hair naturally.

"You really want to know," Hubble said, "it was like a reflex. I mean, I was right behind the door, with the knife. They came through, Joyce came first. So I grabbed her. I mean, I figured she was setting me up. And maybe she was . . ." He tightened his grip in Joyce Trigstadt's hair. "Who knows?"

"I didn't even know you were here," the woman breathed. "How could I know? I—"

"What you should be doing, Claude," Hastings broke in, "is thinking ahead."

"Yeah, well, I'm doing a whole lot of thinking, don't worry. I'm—"

"There's only two ways this can go," Hastings said. "Either we cut you loose, or we hold on to you. And you know the answer to that one. You know you're going to jail. The only question is, how much trouble are you going to cause us between now and then? You understand what I'm saying—what I'm *really* saying?"

Hubble made no response. But his eyes were watchful.

"What I'm really saying is that this thing can go two ways—either a domestic dispute, or a big hostage drama. You understand?"

Still no response. But still their eyes were locked.

"You want to make a big deal of it, that's fine. Like you say, there're people with guns out there. So you can probably get on the six-o'clock news, if that's what you want. Or else you can be smart, do it the easy way. You don't have a gun, just a knife. So right there, that's a plus for you. I mean, an assault rifle, then

197

that'd be a problem. But a knife . . ." Once more, dismissively, Hastings waved his cocked pistol.

"Either way," he continued, "you're going to jail—or the morgue, if some rookie gets spooked. Which one, jail or the morgue, that depends on you, on how you decide to play it. Let's say you play it smart. Let's say, in about fifteen minutes, you hand over the knife. Right there, you've saved the city a lot of trouble—and expense. So we take you downtown, all very calm, very low-key. Then we talk." A heavily laden moment passed. "We talk about Collingwood."

Having pronounced the fateful word, Hastings paused again, looking for a reaction. Would Hubble acknowledge the significance of Collingwood?

"You tell us why it happened, on Collingwood. We know someone hired you. You're not looking for kicks. You're a businessman, and we want the name of your employer. So if you give us a name, then right away you've done yourself a lot of good. You've also saved the city a major hassle. So we tell the DA about how you gave up the knife, and how you cooperated and gave us a name. And we—"

"It was an accident. It wasn't meant to be murder." Hubble spoke softly, intensely. For the first time, he looked steadily into Hastings's eyes. Finally they'd come to the truth.

Hastings nodded encouragement, at the same time drawing a straightback chair up to face Hubble across the cluttered coffee table, with Collier to his left. For the first time he could see that, even though she'd lowered her weapon, her grip on the gun was white-knuckled. Collier's reserves were drawing taut. Her eyes did not leave the knife that now rested flat against Joyce Trigstadt's neck.

"An accident." Hastings spoke quietly, speculatively. Signifying that the final bargaining had begun. "You were hired to work Hardaway over. But he wasn't supposed to die." It was a soft-spoken statement, not a question.

"When he fell, he hit his head on the curb."

Hastings nodded. Frowning, apparently deep in thought, he let a long moment pass as he glanced covertly at Collier, then looked again at Hubble. Now Hastings's manner was earnest, entirely forthcoming:

"Let's suppose you put away your knife and we put away our guns. Then let's suppose the three of us walk out of here. There's no threats, no anger, nothing. We just go out into the hallway, and we say everything's cool. Then we—"

"What about Joyce?" Hubble asked.

"She stays here. She's out of it." Hastings turned to Joyce Trigstadt. Saying: "You can clean up, have a drink, whatever. We'll get a locksmith out here this evening, and tomorrow we'll replace your door. All we want from you now is silence. As far as you're concerned, there never was a knife. Hubble was here, but the four of us were just talking. Got it?"

"But—"

Collier spoke to the other woman: "Put some peroxide on that cut, and comb your hair over it. You'll be fine."

"The three of us," Hastings went on, speaking to Hubble, "will go downstairs and get into a police van. We'll go downtown, and you'll get booked, everything by the numbers. But the charge isn't murder. The charge is aggravated assault. Or, worst case, manslaughter. And instead of adding great bodily harm and obstruction of justice and God knows whatever else we could come up with, we just forget about the last hour or two, because you were cooperative." He smiled. "How's that sound, Claude?"

"It sounds too good to be true. It also sounds like I'm trusting you with my black ass. Which I'm not about to do."

199

"You don't have a choice, Claude. I'm all you've got. Either we make a deal now—right now—or we do it the hard way. It's your call. If you use that knife, you'll die right in this room. If that doesn't happen, then you could die in the gas chamber. That's one way. The other way, you give us the names we want, and we all go downtown and you get booked for an aggravated assault on Collingwood on the night of Tuesday, May ninth. You choose."

Hubble stared one last time at Hastings before he disentangled his fingers from Joyce Trigstadt's hair, shoved her away. As she flung herself blindly from the couch, Hubble calmly wiped the blade of the knife on the couch. He folded the knife closed, slipped it into the sheath on his belt. Reciprocating, Hastings holstered his revolver, nodded for Collier to holster the Glock.

"Before you get dressed," Hastings said, "I want names."

"I thought we did that downtown."

Hastings shook his head. "Wrong. You give us the names now. Downtown, we talk about it—about how it all came down. But we need the names now, to show good faith."

"A lawyer," Hubble said. "We go downtown, I need a lawyer."

"No problem. Speaking of which . . ." Hastings read the suspect his Miranda rights, with Collier witnessing. In the bedroom, door closed, Joyce Trigstadt was crying loudly. After Hubble received his rights, he sighed, deeply resigned. He muttered fervently, "Ah, shit."

Still seated, Collier looked thoughtfully at the slim, dramatically muscled man sitting on the room's only couch in his white underwear. Finally she said, "I checked out your record yesterday, Claude. You've been arrested three times, but you've never fallen. Right?"

"Yeah. Right." Once more, Hubble sighed deeply.

"And you've never been involved in anything like this before. Murder—you've never been arrested for—"

"*Jesus*, it wasn't murder." Angrily, hands spread, plaintively, he appealed to Hastings: "I thought we had a deal. I thought—"

"I'm not talking about Collingwood, Claude," Collier said. "I'm talking about your record. And I'm telling you that the lieutenant is making you a hell of a deal. Because even if you don't beat the aggravated assault charge, or maybe manslaughter, you'll still have only one felony conviction on your record. Which means that if you ever decide to make something of your life, you'll have a shot. Especially if the DA asks for a suspended sentence."

"Which can happen," Hastings said, "if you cooperate."

"If I cop, you mean," Hubble said bitterly.

"Call it what you want," Collier countered. "What I'm telling you is, you look to me like you're smart. You look like a winner to me. Not a loser."

"But if you don't give us those names now," Hastings said, "right now, then you're a loser."

"What happened to our deal? I put up my knife, everything's cool. We walk out together, no guns. We get in the van together, that's what you said."

"That hasn't changed," Collier said. "The part about the names hasn't changed, either. It's just that we want them up front. Someone's got to go first. And you're it."

"Aw, shit." He punched the sofa, hard. "*Shit.*"

In the silence, Hastings and Collier waited. Finally, with his eyes cast down, he muttered, "Delbert Gay, he's the one. He's a low-life private eye. He's the one."

Hastings nodded. "I know Delbert Gay."

"Well, he's the one."

"He hired you."

"Right."

"For how much?"

"A thousand."

"Why'd he hire you? Why'd he want Charles Hardaway worked over?"

"He didn't say. And I didn't ask."

"Someone hired him. Delbert Gay was the middleman."

Hubble shrugged. "Probably."

"So the question is, who hired Delbert Gay?"

Hubble's eyes shifted warily, but he made no reply.

"You know who hired Gay," Collier said. "Don't you?"

"No."

"You're lying, Claude. Don't lie to us. Everything changes, if you lie. Everything's off."

"I'm *not* lying. I *don't* know."

"But you suspect," Hastings said. "You have an idea."

"You talk about the DA. You going to tell him what I suspect? He going to court with something I suspect?" Contemptuously, he shook his head. "Shit."

"You're quite a student of the law."

"I try."

"I'm going to give you a name. If he's the one you suspect, you tell us. Understand?"

No reply.

"The name is Bruce Weston. He's a lawyer."

Resigned, Hubble shrugged, then nodded. "Yeah, he's the one."

"We get downtown, you tell us how you know his name. Understood?"

"Understood."

"All right. Get dressed."

35

"There." Hastings pointed. "In the loading zone."

Canelli turned the cruiser into the loading zone, set the brake, switched off the engine.

"You think Weston'll see us?" Canelli asked.

"He knows we're coming. I doubt he'll want a couple of cops cluttering up his fancy waiting room for very long."

"Could you fill me in, Lieutenant? I mean, I don't know how much Hubble said yesterday."

"We made a deal. He admitted that Delbert Gay hired him to work Hardaway over. He also testified that on at least one occasion, he carried a package of what was probably money to Gay from Weston. And he saw Weston and Gay together twice during the period we're talking about. In other words, Hubble cooperated. So he gets to cop. He'll plead to aggravated assault on Hardaway in exchange for giving us Gay and Weston. The DA will raise the charge to manslaughter, and they'll get a co-operative judge."

"But what about yesterday? Cutting his girlfriend."

"The girl'll go along, won't press charges. Collier is holding her hand today, getting her door fixed, buying her lunch, things like that."

"So the cutting never happened." Canelli's swarthy face softened into a conspiratorial grin. "False alarm."

"I want Weston and whoever gives Weston his orders. Hubble's a little fish."

"Do you think this thing could go all the way up to Harold Best, Lieutenant? Is that what you're thinking?"

"Him and others. His wife, and her father. His campaign manager, too. Sobel."

"Jeez, this is pretty heavy stuff, Lieutenant. I mean, I just read an article saying Harold Best is the golden boy of American politics."

"To me, he looked like a spoiled kid who never grew up." Hastings glanced at his watch. Nine o'clock on a cold, foggy morning in San Francisco's financial district: wind-whipped concrete canyons, well-dressed minions of the marketplace hunched against the cold. "Ready?" he asked.

"Ready."

"I am amazed," Weston said. "Truly amazed. My God, you know Delbert Gay's a certified liar. He'll say anything—incriminate anyone—if there's a dollar to be made."

"He's admitted that he hired Claude Hubble to attack Hardaway. And he's admitted that you hired him to get the job done."

"And you believe him."

"Yessir, I do."

Sitting behind his outsize desk, with his back to his prime view of San Francisco Bay, Weston shook his head incredulously as he fixed Hastings with a pitying stare. "You're in over your head, Lieutenant. I hope you haven't gone to the DA with this story. He'll laugh you out of his office."

"Do you have connections with Harold Best or any of his people?"

"You mean *the* Harold Best? The senatorial candidate?"

Was it guarded surprise that Hastings saw in the other man's face? Caution? Something else?

"That's right. *The* Harold Best."

"Then the answer is no. All I know about Harold Best is what I read on the cover of *Time.*"

"His staff? His managers?"

"No. Why do you ask?"

"At first," Hastings said, "we didn't have a motive for the Hardaway murder. We thought it was just a random gay-bashing. But now we know that Charles Hardaway was killed because he was blackmailing Harold Best."

No response. But behind his gold-rimmed designer glasses, Bruce Weston's improbably blue eyes were speculative. Resting on the desk, his hands were contracting into loose fists.

"So what I want from you," Hastings said, "is the name of whoever hired you to order the attack on Hardaway."

"I've got nothing to say."

"You're a criminal lawyer, Mr. Weston. You know how the game is played. I'll give up a little fish to get a bigger fish. I made a deal with Hubble to get Delbert Gay. And I'm giving up Gay to get you. If you cooperate, I'll make the same deal with you. Tell me who told you to take Hardaway out, and you've got a free ride."

Weston's well-bred snort was contemptuous. "You're incredible, Lieutenant. How do you know the office isn't wired?"

"I figure this isn't a conversation you want on tape."

A frosty amusement touched the corners of Weston's mouth. "Let's suppose," he said, "that I do decide to make a deal. I don't mean to insult you, Lieutenant, but any deal I make, it'd be with, say, a deputy chief."

Hastings shrugged. "Suit yourself. I'll be happy to set it up. You should know, though, that if you do business with me, you've got a better chance of keeping the deal quiet."

As he'd done during their first interview, Weston rose and went to his window, standing with his back to the two detectives. Catching Hastings's eye, Canelli smiled, nodded cheerful encouragement, turned up an optimistic thumb.

Finally, still with his back turned, Weston said, "At first— the first few months—all I was asked to do was get money to Charles Hardaway. Period."

"You didn't ask why?"

"In politics, at these levels, one never asks why. *Never.*" As he said it, Weston turned to face them. In the few minutes he had stood looking out the window, his face, at first so urbanely composed, had become haggard, visibly etched with fear. It was a dramatic transformation.

"Did Sobel pay you for getting the money to Hardaway?"

Weston shook his head in asperity. "You don't understand. With people like the Bests, you don't take money from them. You do them favors. Then they do you favors. No money ever changes hands."

"So," Hastings said, "you handled the payoffs to Hardaway. As a favor to the Bests—or maybe Forster?" Weston looked at Hastings as if he'd touched a nerve.

"And then," Canelli said, "Sobel told you to hit Hardaway. Another little favor."

"If by 'hit' you mean kill, then the answer is no. He wanted Hardaway worked over, that's all. It was meant as a warning. Nothing more."

"So you took care of it," Canelli said.

"I took care of it."

"Have you talked to Sobel since the murder?"

"Twice. On the phone. Once immediately after I learned that Hardaway had been killed. Then I called Sobel again, when I got word that you'd questioned Delbert Gay."

"What was the second call about?"

"It was to say that we could be in trouble. I identified myself as Robert Brown, which was a code we'd agreed on if there were problems."

"How'd he respond?" Canelli asked.

Weston shrugged. "Minimally. A few words, nothing more."

"When I first interrogated you," Hastings said, "did you think you might be in trouble?"

Frowning, Weston considered the question. Then, thoughtfully: "Not really. To be honest, I thought I'd run right over you. As it turns out . . ." He smiled ruefully. Repeating: "As it turns out, I was wrong."

"As it turns out," Hastings said, "you were."

36

"My God," Friedman said, "this gives new meaning to 'white-collar crime.' " Then, ostensibly as an afterthought and actually as a rare compliment, Friedman said: "I'm impressed that you opened Weston up. He must not know that the case against Hubble is pretty shaky without any physical evidence or any witness that can identify him."

"He knew we'd opened up Delbert Gay, don't forget."

"Except that Gay'll probably die before he can testify in court."

"Maybe Weston doesn't know Gay is dying."

Friedman nodded thoughtfully as he drew a cigar from the pocket of an ash-smudged vest. He allowed himself two cigars a day, usually smoked in Hastings's office while the two co-

commanders discussed tactics. Pointedly, Hastings did not provide an ashtray. As a result, much to Hastings's annoyance, Friedman flicked his cigar ashes into the wastebasket.

"So," Friedman said as he began reflectively to unwrap the cigar, "we've got the net spread." He found matches in another pocket, lit the cigar, and tossed the still-smoking match into the wastebasket. Stoically, Hastings stared after it as Friedman settled back in his chair. Hastings recognized the portents. Friedman was about to pontificate: "Since Hardaway managed to contact Best without telling Randy, the odds are he went through Best's campaign organization. He obviously got to So-bel. Who, let's assume, realizes he has a very, very hot political potato on his hands, and he's got to get rid of it. So what can he do? There's only one reasonable course of action: he contacts someone with real authority. Who, when you think about it, has to be either Best himself or his wife. Or, on top of the pyramid, James Forster."

"Right." Hastings realized that Friedman was speaking tentatively, almost reluctantly. Why? Was it the mention of names that represented enough political power to ruin him? Was that the bottom line?

"Let's assume," Friedman said, "that Sobel tells Carolyn Best there's a blackmail problem. That'd be logical. In the chain of command, Carolyn would probably be Sobel's immediate superior. So let's say she agrees: they've got a major PR problem. Then let's assume that she decides to pay Hardaway off, accedes to his demands. For a few months, everything's cool. Hardaway collects his money, which the Bests don't really miss. But then Hardaway gets greedy. He threatens to go public with what he knows unless he gets a lot more money. Carolyn is suddenly in over her head. She goes to her father. Maybe she admits that she screwed up, maybe not. In any case, Forster decides to have Hardaway worked over, as a warning. If Hardaway doesn't take the hint, then they'll have him killed. To people like Forster, people like Hardaway are nothing more than insects."

"If we tackle Forster, we do it together. Right?" Hastings asked.

"Right," Friedman replied.

"When?"

"How about tomorrow? We fly down first thing in the morning."

"Saturday?" Hastings frowned.

"I'll set the whole thing up," Friedman said. "We'll meet at the airport in the morning."

"Will we be working with the LAPD?"

"No. This is all off the record."

"You think that's smart?"

"Smart, I don't know. But it could be fun."

"Fun?"

"Fun."

37

When she heard her son's door open, Janet Collier unconsciously braced herself. For the last half hour, with the telephone cord trailing under his closed door, Charlie had been talking to Gordon Browne, his most trusted friend. Now, at eight o'clock on a warm Friday evening, Charlie was advancing down the hallway to the living room. His stride was purposeful.

"Gordon wants me to stay over. Tomorrow his dad's taking him to the Sports and Boat Show at the Cow Palace. I can go with them."

"What about your game tomorrow?"

"I'd rather go to the Cow Palace."

"But you're starting at second base."

"Gordon's dad promised they'd get two jet scooters, though,

for when they go on vacation. He might even buy them tomorrow, at the show."

She experienced a brief, recognizable pang of envy. An office machine salesman, Alfred Browne regularly earned six figures in commissions. Lois, his wife, taught special education classes. Gordon, age fourteen and indulged, was their only child. Whenever the two mothers met, invariably to arrange activities for their sons, Lois Browne always managed to suggest that she didn't consider police work suitable for women.

Finally Janet said, "If you really want to stay over at Gordon's, it's okay. But you really should think about it, Charlie. You've practiced hard all spring. And your hitting, especially, is great. Which is why Ray wants you to start tomorrow."

"Yeah, well, I've only been to the Sports and Boat Show twice in my whole life." In his voice she could hear an edge that could mean trouble. Beyond all doubt, Gordon Browne made the Sports and Boat Show every year.

"Charlie . . ." Janet rose from the couch, went to him, looked down into his eyes. He stood in the entrance to the hallway with his legs spread wide, unconsciously bracing for confrontation. His eyes were hazel, like hers.

"Tomorrow's opening day for the season. And you're starting at second. That's a big deal, Charlie. It's something you've worked for—hard. I think you should consider that."

"And besides," she might have said, "I want to see you play. I want to root for you, Charlie. I want to yell my head off."

For a short but definitive moment, he made no reply; in his eyes she saw an almost imperceptible flicker of hesitation. This flicker, she knew, was her edge. But how to capitalize on it? "When you're older, you'll understand"? Would that work? To herself, she shook her head. No. If she'd read the flicker of hesitation correctly, he'd realized that he should play second base tomorrow. But how could he play ball without appearing to admit his mother was right?

Could she help him save face? Certainly, it was worth a try. "When's the boat show run?" she asked. "All weekend?"

He nodded cautiously.

"Well, tomorrow's Saturday. Why don't you play ball tomorrow? Then, on Sunday, you and I can go to the boat show. We'll go in the afternoon, and afterwards we'll have pizza."

"I'd rather have Kentucky Fried."

Realizing that the demand was tactical, she debated the wisdom of conceding. Finally she said, "We'll see."

For a final moment he held his position, also a tactical maneuver. Then: "Gordon's still on the phone." He turned away, walked down the hallway to his room. One more mother-son confrontation resolved.

She returned to the couch, eyed the silent TV, eyed the paperback of Toni Morrison's *Beloved,* open face-down on the couch. Was she up to a few more pages of Morrison's incredibly dense, compelling prose? *Beloved,* the story of a mother's love, a mother's guilt, finally a mother's defeat.

From the hallway, she heard Charlie's door open. He would be returning the phone to its shelf in the hallway. And, yes, he would now return to his room and the TV. In an hour or two, she would suggest that he go to bed early, because of the game tomorrow. He wouldn't take her advice. But he would expect her to offer it. The game started tomorrow at nine o'clock. Sharp.

At nine o'clock tomorrow, the two lieutenants, Friedman and Hastings, would be on their way to Los Angeles. Frank had waited until four o'clock to tell her. She'd been Xeroxing a summary of the Hardaway homicide. The Xerox machine, one of several, was in the basement of the Hall of Justice, next to the

213

cafeteria. With the copies collated, she'd stopped in the cafeteria for a cup of coffee. At four o'clock, the cafeteria had been almost deserted. Someone had left a newspaper on one of the tables, and she was sipping coffee and reading the paper when she realized that someone was standing beside her. Frank.

"How about a doughnut," he'd said, "to go with the coffee?" Caught unaware, she'd smiled up at him—not the official smile she'd trained herself to greet him with, but the intimate, female-male smile that was always her first instinct whenever they met.

He brought the doughnuts, refilled her cup of decaf from the cafeteria urn, filled his own cup, then sat facing her—and smiled deep into her eyes.

"Hardaway?" he asked, pointing to the stack of Xeroxes.

Carefully unsmiling, she nodded.

"My report on what happened in Los Angeles—it's almost finished. First of the week, it'll be done."

She nodded again. Her eyes strayed to the rear of the cafeteria, where two Bunco inspectors were talking over empty coffee cups. One of the men, Brian Russ, was staring at her. Before she'd made Homicide, when she was in Bunco, Russ had briefly been her partner. Meaningfully, Russ nodded to her, quizzically raising his eyebrows. The implied question: Had she gotten into Homicide on her back—with Hastings on top?

For almost an hour, facing each other across the cafeteria table, they talked about the Hardaway homicide—and about Hastings's trip to Los Angeles. In detail, he described the sequence of events: the conversation with Sobel, the go-go campaign manager, followed by the interview with Carolyn Best. Followed, finally, by the confrontation with Harold Best, almost certainly California's next United States senator. As he

214

talked, Frank's manner changed. He became more animated—less the calm, stoic policeman, more an ordinary starstruck citizen who'd brushed shoulders with celebrities.

Listening to him, questioning him, she tried to control the envy she felt—and, yes, the frustration. She was the officer of record on the case. Frank was her superior officer. As long as the case had appeared to be nothing more than a street crime or a gay-bashing gone wrong, she'd been free to work the case as she pleased.

But then, when the trail had led to Bruce Weston, Hastings had taken over. Hastings, and now Friedman. Tomorrow, while she was watching Charlie play second base, the two detectives would be on their way to Los Angeles. Objective: to interrogate James Forster.

Frank was apologetic. Yes, protocol dictated that he should have taken the officer of record to Los Angeles, even if only as a witness during interrogations. And, yes, he and Friedman had talked about it. But, he admitted, "it just wouldn't've worked."

Meaning that squadroom gossip would have them shacked up together in Los Angeles.

Meaning that, because she was a woman—because, yes, she and Lieutenant Frank Hastings were attracted to each other—she'd been denied her professional rights.

And Frank had let it happen.

Very deliberately, she put her coffee cup down, turned both ways to make sure they couldn't be overheard. Then, furious, her eyes locked with his, she spoke in a voice both soft and yet so tight it caught in her throat: "I guess it isn't the time or the place," she said, "but I've got to tell you this. I don't have a choice. I'm not going to leave here without telling you—speaking my piece."

"I know what you're going to say. And—"

She raised an angry hand, silenced him. "This whole thing between us is crazy. We held hands once at the scene of a crime, we once kissed each other in the police parking garage, and we drank tea in a Chinese restaurant while we admitted that, if you weren't already in a relationship, and if I didn't have a son and a mother who need me, then we'd probably be lovers, you and I. That same night, if we'd been free, we could've gone to a motel. God knows, I would've done it. Except that Charlie was expecting me to cook his dinner, and Ann was cooking dinner for you. So we did the right thing, you and I—the honorable thing. We said good-bye. We didn't kiss each other good-bye—we *said* good-bye. It was like a Jane Austen novel, what we did. It's—God—it's *Victorian*. We've hardly kissed each other. But those goddam jerks in the squadroom, they've got us in bed together. They—"

"You're wrong," he said. "That's not what they think."

"It *is* what they think. Otherwise, you'd've taken me to Los Angeles with you."

He didn't reply directly, didn't deny it. He only looked at her with his somber brown eyes. As if he were bewildered, he slowly shook his head, saying, "My God, it's like we're teenagers. That's the way I feel. Except that I wouldn't be saying this, if I was a teenager. I'd be too shy."

In spite of herself, she smiled. "You haven't said anything, Frank. I've been doing all the talking. You've just been listening—and looking sheepish."

His first reaction was irritation. Followed, almost immediately, by a rueful, aw-shucks smile. But then, speaking slowly and somberly, musing, he said, "If I lived alone, there wouldn't be a problem."

"Except that you'd be living alone."

"But we'd have a place to go, the two of us. We'd have my place."

"I don't want to be the one who breaks up your relationship, Frank. I've never met Ann. But she and I are single moms. We're both trying to raise teenagers without fathers. And that's hard enough, without someone stealing your man."

"Jesus, talk about Victorian novels. Is that the way you're thinking about this—that you're *stealing* me?"

"I'm just saying that—"

"I like Ann. I respect her—all those things that you're supposed to feel for someone. But whatever it is, it isn't love. It's—in a way, the whole thing was an accident that we're living together. We'd been dating for about a year. I had a place in the Marina, and once a week, generally, she'd come over. Sometimes we'd eat in, sometimes we'd go out. Sometimes Ann's ex-husband took her boys for weekends, and Ann and I might go away overnight. Or she'd come over to my place for the weekend. That didn't happen often, though."

"Did you go to her place overnight?"

"Never when the boys were there. When she was first divorced, Ann tried that a couple of times—had men stay over. It didn't work. Once, in fact, it was a disaster."

"The more you talk," she said, "the more Ann sounds like me—maybe like most single moms. The first year or two after you've divorced, you go crazy. At least I did. I thought I had to have sex. It's all I thought about—finding a man, making love. But then there was Charlie. Parenthood, in other words. And there was my mom, too. A few times, when Charlie was little, I'd have my mom baby-sit while I slept over at some guy's house, mostly on Friday or Saturday. But my mom didn't like it. She isn't a prude, that's not it. She just has the absolute conviction that if a couple screws up their marriage—well—it hap-

217

pens. But then they've got to take care of their children. Love is a mystery, she used to say. But raising a kid, that's no mystery. That's hard work."

"Your mom—it sounds like she makes a lot of sense."

"She *does* make a lot of sense. She also knows whereof she speaks. She was divorced twice."

"You're an only child?"

She nodded. "You, too?"

He nodded, then asked, "Does your mom live alone?"

"Yes. She doesn't like it, and she doesn't make much money, so she doesn't have much left for pleasure. But she married once purely for money, and she swore she'd never do it again."

"So you help her out."

"I help her, and she helps me."

"Baby-sitting. Looking after Charlie when you pull extra duty."

She nodded.

"The first two years, did you ever bring men home?"

"A couple of times, on weekends."

"Did Charlie mind?"

"Yes, he minded. A lot."

"Does he ever get to see his father?"

"His father," she answered bitterly, "is in Pittsburgh. He married a woman with two children, but they're divorced. It's been three years since I heard from him. And then he wanted to borrow money."

Because he knew about her marriage, he only shook his head contemptuously. Then he said, "I want to finish telling you about Ann and me."

"I'm not sure I want to hear it."

"I realize that. But I want to tell you."

She made no reply. Allowing him to say, "After almost two

years, Ann and I had pretty much settled into a once-a-week rut. We never talked about it, but we knew that's what it was: a rut. Separately, we wondered what would happen if I moved in with her. But it was never discussed. Not until I made the mistake of getting my skull fractured during an arrest. I was in the hospital for a week, and then I was told to go home and stay in bed for two more weeks."

"But you didn't go home. You went to Ann's. And you stayed."

Surprised, he raised his eyes to hers. "How'd you know?"

She only smiled. It was a wistful smile, shadowed by vague regret. Then she glanced at her watch. They'd been talking for almost an hour. During that time, a handful of their fellow inspectors had come and gone. Some of them had looked and smiled and nodded; others had looked discreetly away as they passed.

"You're right," he answered. "I stayed. Ann has a big Victorian flat on Green Street, a great place. It's only two bedrooms, though. For the first week Ann slept on the living room couch. Then she moved into the bedroom. It was something else we never really talked about. She just left her pillow on the bed one night, instead of taking it into the living room."

"So you stayed—and stayed." Once more, she spoke wistfully.

His sigh, too, was faintly wistful.

"Right."

"Her children—how'd they react?"

"No problem. They're boys, fourteen and sixteen. I think they like having me around. Especially since I keep my mouth shut whenever there's a family argument."

"But now you want to leave."

"I've told you why I—"

"I think," she cut in, "that you'd make a mistake leaving. Living alone—it's no fun."

"I wouldn't be alone, though. There'd be you, sometimes."

"Frank . . ." Involuntarily, she touched his hand. "I can't give you any promises. You know that. It's like my mother said. Love is a mystery."

"I'm not asking for any promises. I'm just trying to tell you that I want some love in my life—some warmth. Some excitement."

This time, her smile was spontaneous. Her laugh was quick, teasing. "I don't think your life lacks for excitement."

"You know what I mean."

"Think about it, before you move out. That's all I'm saying."

"You say you won't go to bed with me, as long as I'm living with Ann. If I believe you, which I do, and if I want you, which I do, then I've got to move out."

"You make it sound like I'm forcing you to move out. But that's not—"

"You're not forcing me to do anything. I know that."

"Ann—does she know what you're thinking?"

"We haven't talked about it. But I think she knows."

"You leave a lot unsaid, you and Ann."

"That's the kind of people we are, when we're together. With you, I'm different. We talk, you and I."

Once more, spontaneously, she touched his hand. She felt him respond. Instantly, the scene that had brought them together came back: the body of a sad little man, her first experience with violent death. And the memory of Frank's kindness had returned.

38

"In my opinion," Friedman said, "Forster is anxious to see us. He must know by now through Sobel or Best that we've got a suspect in custody, but doesn't know anything beyond that, all according to plan. So we've got them guessing. We—*there.*" He pointed ahead, to the freeway sign. "There it is—Mulholland Drive. That's our off-ramp. Go west on Mulholland." He consulted his Los Angeles map as Hastings signaled for the turn.

After he'd negotiated the merge onto Mulholland, Hastings asked, "Did you talk to Forster himself when you called yesterday?"

Friedman nodded. "I had to go through a secretary, but it wasn't a problem. It's like I said—I think he wants to see us, decide which way he thinks we'll jump."

"So which way *will* we jump?"

"That," Friedman said, "is why we came to Los Angeles, to figure out which way we jump. If we aren't sure, then neither is Forster. Which has got to be a plus."

"Why do I get the feeling that maybe this trip isn't really necessary? Why do I think this is sport for you?"

Friedman's smile was amiable. "You could have a point. I think golf is silly, and I'm too fat for tennis. I don't fish, and I don't collect stamps."

"But you love to stick it to fat cats."

"That's true, I do—*pompous* fat cats. I love to prick them, watch them deflate."

"This," Forster said, "is remarkable. It's absolutely unprecedented in my experience. And I must tell you, gentlemen, that at my age, with a very full life behind me, there isn't much left that's unprecedented." As if he were thanking them for the pleasure they were giving him, Forster smiled genially. He was a slim, athletic man of medium height and girth. His face glowed with ruddy good health. His hair was thick and white, carefully cut, casually styled. The eyes were a clear, shrewd gray. The mustache, carefully trimmed, was his only suggestion of vanity. Countless lines and wrinkles seamed the face, making a pattern that was the product of consistent good fortune. Seated behind a desk covered with piles of neatly stacked papers, James Forster projected an intense air of engagement. Although the smile came easily and often, the eyes were constantly calculating and recalculating, relentlessly probing. He wore a white knit polo shirt with his initials stitched on the left breast. The open collar revealed a sagging neck that was the only hint of age's effects. Beneath the desk, Hastings could see white duck trousers and white sneakers, suggesting that Forster meant to go sailing after their interview was concluded. Or could it be tennis?

Forster's office was just as full as his desk, and just as functional. Every shelf and tabletop overflowed with books and papers, most of them printouts. One wall of the office was almost entirely glass, offering a prime view of the nearby wooded hills of Coldwater Canyon, with the blue of the Pacific in the background. They were high enough to look down on the yellow layer of smog that covered the Los Angeles Basin's flatlands to the east.

Forster turned to Hastings, saying, "I know about your foray last Wednesday. I was surprised that you didn't try to contact me."

Hastings expected the gambit and was ready with a response: "After talking to your daughter and son-in-law, I figured I had to go back to San Francisco for instructions." He gestured to Friedman, seated beside him. "He's the boss."

"Oh?" Genially smiling, Forster turned his attention to Friedman. Then the smile faded, replaced by a slight, polite frown. "But you're both lieutenants."

"We're co-commanders," Friedman said. "However, I'm senior. Which means that I sit in my office and theorize, while Lieutenant Hastings is out in the field risking his neck."

Forster smiled again, this time appreciatively. "Ah." He nodded. "Yes, I see." Then, after a glance at his watch, Forster's manner hardened. All business now: "I know, of course, why you're here. I've talked to both Harold and my daughter. So we can dispense with the preliminaries." Seeking confirmation, he looked at each detective in turn. Taking his cue from Friedman, Hastings nodded agreement.

"In your, ah, profession," Forster said, "I imagine you've often been involved with situations like this, where you come into possession of information that, if it's made public, could cause considerable damage." He looked at both detectives. This time neither man reacted. Could this be the prelude to the offer of a bribe?

"Just so we understand each other," Forster said, "I'm referring to the unhappy fact that, when they were in college, Harold and Randy Carpenter had a brief homosexual affair. They were discreet about it, though, and there was seemingly no harm done. Harold went on to make a spectacular success of his life. As you know."

"The rumors are," Friedman said, "that you made Harold Best what he is today. He's your creation. Yours, and your daughter's."

Almost fondly now, Forster smiled benignly at Friedman. "I'm aware of those rumors, and I'm gratified to say that, in general, they're true. Harold is a type that is not uncommon in politics. He's suggestible on the one hand, and yet he's also ego-driven. But it's an ego that's a function of vanity, and therefore translates into deep personal insecurities. Unlike the ego one finds in the business world, to take an example. The businessman's ego is predatory. Fully expressed, the ego-driven businessman would use a broadsword to deal with his rivals. But for people like Harold the ego is a shield, something to hide behind. At bottom, Harold is a cowering child, a weakling lost in a world of 'let's pretend.' It's a syndrome that often afflicts actors."

"On Wednesday," Hastings said, "he didn't seem like a weakling. He accused me of extortion, among other things."

"Harold can be peevish, certainly, especially when he's frightened. But he's not a fighter. On the other hand," Forster said, "I am a fighter. A predator, if you will. My ego drives me to destroy my enemies, not hide from them. Do you understand the distinction?"

"Oh, yes." Hastings nodded. "I understand."

"Likewise," Friedman said. His face, Hastings saw, was utterly inscrutable and absorbed. They were playing Friedman's favorite game, a one-winner contest of wits.

"So," Forster said, "let's put the cards on the table. Agreed?"

The two detectives nodded agreement.

"First, we've got the Carpenter problem. If he goes public, then Harold's career is finished. That's a given." Forster's manner was uninflected, as if he were discussing a mathematical theorem.

"Have there been other homosexual episodes?" Friedman asked. "Since Carpenter?"

"I suspect there were. A few, perhaps, but they are not at issue here." Forster's voice was calm, revealing nothing of his feelings. His eyes, like Friedman's, were unreadable. "Carpenter himself is no threat. Even if Harry should leave off paying him, I don't think Carpenter would call the *National Enquirer*. He's got too much pride."

"But then," Hastings said, "there was Charles Hardaway."

"Which is," Friedman joined in, his voice silky, "why we're here. Your problems with Carpenter are your affair. We came because of Hardaway—because he was murdered."

Forster's reply came smoothly, convincingly: "As far as I can determine, Hardaway found out about Harold and Randy. And, yes, Hardaway decided to try his hand at blackmail. Apparently he simply contacted the campaign with what he called a 'sensational story.' That got him all the way up to Barton Sobel. You met Bart." He looked inquiringly at Hastings, who nodded.

"Apparently Bart decided he could handle the problem himself. He gave Hardaway twenty-five thousand dollars and told him to get lost."

"But he didn't get lost," Friedman said. "He came back for more. The closer the election got, the more dangerous he became. Until finally you had to have him killed."

With his hands clasped on the desk, head slightly bowed, Forster seemed to consider the accusation, his manner as grave as a magistrate's. Finally he said, "Since you came to town on Wednesday, Lieutenant Hastings, I've made it my business to inform myself on this matter. I've spent hours in consultation with my lawyer. And I'm completely satisfied that I know the truth."

"Yes," Hastings said, "I'm sure you've worked out a story."

Ignoring the other man's sarcasm, Forster spoke calmly: "It's true that Hardaway was blackmailing the campaign. And it's true that Bart Sobel paid him off. It was, of course, a mistake. Blackmailers are voracious. On the other hand, twenty-five thousand dollars was, after all, not much more than petty cash, in a campaign."

"So what you're saying," Friedman said, "is that Sobel acted on his own when he decided to pay off Hardaway."

"Yes."

"Did Sobel also make the decision to have Hardaway killed?"

Forster's response was a shake of the head and a lugubrious sigh, as if he regretted the necessity of dealing with a backward student: "There was no decision to kill Hardaway, Lieutenant, as you should very well know. Neither was there a decision to have him beaten. It was a random gay-bashing that went wrong. From our point of view, admittedly, the timing was fortuitous. But that doesn't mean we ordered Hardaway killed. It was a coincidence, no more, no less."

"We believe," Friedman said, "that when you decided Charles Hardaway had to be killed, Sobel got in touch with Bruce Weston, a criminal lawyer in San Francisco. You probably don't know Weston, and I'm sure Sobel didn't enlighten you. He'd want to keep you ignorant of his plans, to protect you. So they agreed on a fee, and Weston took the job. He contacted a sleazy private investigator who, in turn, hired a professional hit man to kill Hardaway."

Forster made no reply. He studied Friedman's face with an expression that was quizzical, faintly amused.

"We've got confessions from all these people." Hastings pressed. "We've got a suspect in custody. He's confessed. He's confessed, and he's implicated the others."

Forster touched a button on his desktop communications console. Moments later, one of the office's two doors opened. Carrying electronic equipment, a young woman entered the room. Ignoring the three men, she placed two black boxes on Forster's desk, one at either end. She flicked two switches, saw two tiny red lights glow. She nodded to Forster, who nodded in return. Moments later, the woman was gone.

"These," Forster said, "as I'm sure you know, are white-noise machines. Jamming devices, in other words, should any of us be wearing a wire. Fair enough?"

"We're not wearing wires," Hastings said.

"Then you won't mind the jamming."

"Not in the least," Friedman answered cheerfully.

"Good." Forster nodded benignly. Then, as formally as if he were speaking from a prepared text, he began:

"It's a phrase that I'm sure you've heard thousands of times. 'You can't do this to me,' the line goes. 'I'm a very important person. I'll have your job if you don't get off my back.' "

The two detectives exchanged knowing glances.

"First," Forster said, "as to the assertion that you've got evidence implicating me in the death of Charles Hardaway, well, I can only conclude that someone paid the assailant to accuse me. To be followed, of course, by the assailant's offer to recant, assuming I'm willing to pay him off. Another blackmail attempt, in other words."

"You don't expect us to respond to that, of course," Friedman said.

"Certainly not. I only bring it up to make the point that I don't pay blackmail. To anyone, even if they're sponsored by the police."

"We should stipulate, though, that Mr. Best is paying off Randy Carpenter. Regularly."

"True," Forster admitted. "But that isn't blackmail under duress. It's Harold's desire that Carpenter receive the money—that Carpenter be provided for."

Friedman decided not to respond.

"Actually," Forster said, "this whole matter comes down to a very simple question: either you investigate Hardaway's death as a random gay-bashing, or you investigate it as a paid attack. Correct?"

The two detectives nodded cautiously.

"If you choose to investigate it as a paid attack, then you'll obviously proceed from the bottom up—from the actual murderer right up to the top. Me, in other words. In the process, my son-in-law's campaign would be a casualty, even if— when—the court throws out the case.

"If, however, you investigate the case as a gay-bashing that went wrong, then there's no reason to involve the Best campaign. You say you have a suspect in custody. I assume he has a lawyer." Expectantly, Forster looked at Friedman, who nodded.

"That lawyer will be authorized to tell the suspect that if he pleads guilty to random gay-bashing, two things would happen. First, he'll receive enhanced legal representation—a first-class lawyer, in other words, available at no expense to the suspect. And, secondly, he'll receive cash in the amount of, say, fifty thousand dollars."

Friedman smiled derisively. "I wondered whether we'd get around to bribery. Don't you think threats will do the job?"

"I've only touched on the threats. However, Lieutenant, my threats are very real, and you should never believe otherwise. One five-minute phone call, and both your careers would be over. Finished. I've no idea how it would be accomplished, or how long it would take. I don't descend to that level. But believe me, it would happen."

As Friedman levered himself forward in his chair, he turned to Hastings, saying, "Time to go, Lieutenant. That was the exit line."

39

"All Hubble has to do," Hastings said, "is recant, say we pressured him to name Delbert Gay and Bruce Weston. Hubble'll say no one hired him. He's a hard-core gay-basher, he'll admit. He's sorry for what he did. Then, surprise, he's got a high-powered lawyer, no questions asked, no bills rendered. And, another surprise, Hubble is fifty thousand dollars richer. The new lawyer, sure as hell, plays golf with the DA. End of the story."

They sat at the far end of the long carved-mahogany bar in the midday anonymity of their hotel. Friedman was drinking Scotch, Hastings seltzer water.

"I've got to admit . . ." Moodily, Friedman sipped the Scotch. "I've got to admit that I'm discouraged. I don't think

I've ever admitted to being discouraged, at least not to you."

Ruefully, Hastings snorted, used his glass to make wet, intricately articulated circles on the bar. "Do you think Forster could really fuck us up, if we go after him? Ruin our careers?"

"I've no doubt," Friedman said. "None at all. I've seen it happen. It takes time, but it happens. The mayor is beholden to the party and the fat cats that put him in office. And the police chief is appointed by the mayor. So one day Forster gives a high-powered buddy a call. 'These two lieutenants,' Forster says, 'they're crossing the line, creating problems. Can you handle it?' No problem, says the friend, who sets up a lunch with the mayor and explains that his honor can't expect much in the way of campaign financing unless Homicide is reorganized. 'After all,' the friend says, 'it's not acceptable for people like us to be embarrassed by people like Hastings and Friedman.' Well, his honor gets the message. So, a few months later, maybe a year later, during the latest departmental shakeup calculated to please the voters, the mayor looks at his organizational chart and discovers that Homicide is supposed to be headed by a captain, not two lieutenants. So he picks a captain who's in line for a favor, and he puts him in charge of Homicide—with orders to make us shape up or ship out. With the accent, of course, on shipping out. Like, to Vice, or Narco."

"I think we should take Hubble to the DA as soon as possible. That's when it'll all come together, when we know whether the DA's going for homicide or manslaughter or something in between. If it's manslaughter, then that'll mean he's not going any higher up the ladder of suspects. If it's murder, then he'd certainly go up the ladder, at least up to Bruce Weston, and probably higher. All the shit hits the fan, then."

"I should remind you," Friedman said, "that we already made a deal with Hubble. 'We'll recommend a charge of aggravated assault to the DA,' we said, 'if you give us Bruce Weston.' If it appears that we welshed—if we recommend murder—not only do we lose Hubble, but we lose credibility with the bad guys. Which would have the effect of drying up about ninety percent of our sources of information. Which we can't afford to have happen. We need Hubble almost as much as he needs us. Plus, if Forster finds out we're going for murder, not assault, he activates his plan to squash us."

"Jesus . . ." Hastings took a drink. "My head aches just thinking about it."

"The sooner we know which way the DA jumps, the sooner we know whether Forster'll actually go after us."

"And whether Hubble is going to show up with a fancy new lawyer and look like someone with fifty thousand under the mattress."

"Have you ever had someone like Forster after you?" Hastings asked.

"I've had threats. Dozens of threats. But I've never actually been hassled. Not that I know of, anyhow. I'm always having problems with the brass, that's no news. But that's built in. I'm a born shit-disturber."

"What I'd like to do"—Hastings glanced at his watch—"I'd like to check out of this hotel, and I'd like to go to the goddam airport, and I'd like to take the goddam shuttle back to San Francisco."

"Likewise. Let's go." They dropped money on the bar and walked to the door.

40

"Thanks, Bart. Thanks for the input." Carolyn Best smiled at the campaign manager. It was a perfunctory smile, a smile of dismissal.

"Yes, Bart," Forster said. He, too, smiled. Impersonally. Also dismissively.

Barton Sobel rose, nodded first to Forster, then to Carolyn Best, finally to Harold Best, who made no response, but looked moodily away. Sobel could hardly remember Best refusing the courtesy of a smile. It was an ominous sign.

When the office door closed on Sobel, Forster rose from behind his desk and strode to the glass wall of his study. At five o'clock on a warm, clear, golden afternoon, the sun was lowering in the sky over the ocean to the west. Already, the horizon was purpling.

Carolyn and Harold Best remained seated side by side on the office's sofa. They hadn't looked at each other or spoken to each other. Separately, their attention was fixed on James Forster, who was finally turning away from the view, striding across the room to his desk. His gaze focused on Carolyn Best.

"Needless to say," Forster began, "I wish I'd known about this situation as it was developing, months ago."

"I wish *I'd* known about it, too," she answered. "Bart didn't tell me until after he'd made the first payment to Hardaway. He exceeded his authority."

Forster shrugged. "Perhaps. Keep in mind, though, that Bart is probably the best in the business, precisely because he's willing to take chances, take the initiative—and, if need be, take the heat. The alternative would have been someone who's constantly asking for direction."

"He paid off a blackmailer without authority. By the time I knew about it, there was damage."

"What would you have done," Forster asked, "if Sobel had asked you for authority?"

"I'd have checked with you," she answered promptly. "However, once the first payoff was made, I decided not to bring you into it. If something went wrong, you could claim complete innocence."

"Meaning that you'd take the heat?"

She shrugged, looked away.

For the first time Harold Best spoke to his wife: "When Bart told you what he'd done, what'd you say?"

"I told him that since he'd taken the initiative, he'd have to live with it. I told him to keep me out of it. And he did, too, initially. But then Hardaway began to get greedy. He began making threats."

"What kind of threats?"

"Jesus, do I have to be explicit?" For a moment she stared at her husband. Then, very softly, she said, "To publish intimate details about you and Randy—do you want me to draw pictures?" She spoke bitterly, viciously.

"So you had Hardaway killed." Harold Best's voice was hardly more than an incredulous whisper. His eyes were averted. Unaware that he was doing it, he began nibbling a fingernail.

Ignoring her husband, Carolyn Best spoke to Forster: "There'd been a few payments when Bart came to me the second time. He realized that he'd made a mistake, and he told me so. One problem was that since he'd set up an elaborate system of cutouts to make the payments, he'd never dealt with Hardaway directly. He had no way of deciding whether Hardaway represented a threat—whether, in fact, he could be scared off. So I decided to take a hand. I got Hardaway's number, and I called him from a phone booth. I identified myself, and told him that if he made any more trouble, he'd be killed. I told him he could have two more payments—twenty-five thousand altogether. But that was all. That was the end. He was paid in the same fashion as Barton used the first time."

"What was his reaction?" Forster asked.

"He seemed stunned." For the first time she looked at her husband fully. "He asked me whether I was really your wife. I suppose a homosexual would naturally doubt that you were married."

Best was looking at his wife intently as he spoke in a low, strained voice. "Yes, I suppose that's so."

"Are you saying," Forster asked his daughter, "that you gave the order to have Hardaway killed without consulting me?"

Quickly, she shook her head. "No, not killed. I never intended that. I threatened Hardaway with murder to get his attention. But I told Sobel to have him beaten. Badly. As a warning."

"It's murder," Best said. "He's dead, for God's sake." His voice was ragged, his eyes haunted. In that moment it seemed impossible that Best could ever again smile for the cameras.

"It was an accident," she answered calmly. "Weston says it's being investigated by the DA as a random gay-bashing that went wrong. The actual assailant will get off with a light sentence, worst case. And he'll be paid for his trouble. Well paid. He'll be—"

"This is incredible," Best broke in. "This is an unbelievable conversation. You're—Christ—you're talking about subverting justice in the basest way. In the campaign we're promising people a better country. A better life. But the two of you, you're—" Unable to find the words, choked by his own outrage, Best broke off. Then, in low, carefully measured words, speaking directly to James Forster, Best said, "Ever since Hastings came, on Wednesday, I've known it would come to this. I—Christ—I've hardly slept. And now . . ." Signifying the end of hope, he gestured loosely, an expression of helpless anguish. "And now, this last hour, it turns out to be worse than I thought. It—it's a—a disaster. It's—"

"Randy will be dead soon," Carolyn said, "and this situation will be resolved."

Best looked hard into his wife's face, but made no response.

Carolyn Best moved impatiently on the couch, signifying that other matters more urgent beckoned. Alert to the movement, and to Forster's corresponding shift—the father and daughter always in sync—Harold Best rose abruptly. As his wife began to rise, frowning, Best restrained her with a gesture. He glanced at Forster. Still seated behind his desk, the older man was watching him carefully. As always, ever alert to even the smallest nuance, Forster was doubtless already anticipating Best's intent.

"About three o'clock this morning," Best began, "lying in bed, I made a decision." He paused, looked at father and daughter in turn. Then, speaking so softly that Forster was forced to lean forward across his desk, hand cupped behind his ear, Best said, "I've decided to quit. I've decided you can have your goddam campaign. I've decided I don't want any more to do with either of you."

Forster's response was mild, measured: "I've got millions sunk into the campaign, Harry. You pull out now, it's larceny. Outright thievery."

"That's bullshit, and you know it. Next year at this time, you'll be worth a lot more than you are now, regardless of this campaign. My campaign—it's sport, for you. It's how you get off."

"Speaking of getting off," Carolyn said, "how do you plan to get off, once you leave? We don't have the most conventional marriage, but we manage. Or, I should say, I manage for both of us."

"I imagine," Forster said, "that Harry will return to his old ways. In fact, I'll predict that he'll move to San Francisco." Forster smiled maliciously. "Am I correct, Harold?"

Gravely, Best nodded. "You're absolutely correct. I don't intend to let Randy die alone."

41

"For once," Esterbrook said, "we agree. Even with physical evidence placing Hubble at the scene, it'd be hard to make a case for murder one. But without physical evidence, even aggravated assault'll be a stretch." Across the desk, the assistant DA looked from Friedman to Hastings, then at Friedman again. Puzzled, he frowned. "Pete, you've got that Cheshire-cat look. You don't mind losing Hubble on murder one?"

"Not if you prosecute for aggravated assault."

"If we prosecute at all, it'll be for manslaughter. Minimum."

"My only interest is in seeing him prosecuted for something. I want him to go to trial."

"I'm trying to figure out what game you're playing. Have you got a deal with Hubble? Is that it?"

"If he falls for manslaughter, that'll do fine."

"We don't have enough for murder, and you don't give a shit. You made a deal," Esterbrook said. "Probably with Hubble. He gives you Weston, and you lay back."

"Probably."

Esterbrook looked at Hastings. Saying: "But what about Pete's Cheshire-cat expression? He's after bigger fish, isn't he?"

"Everyone needs a hobby," Friedman answered airily.

"Before I sign off on this, I need to know your game plan. Top to bottom."

"Top to bottom," Friedman said, "Hubble goes to trial for manslaughter, if that's what it takes. He takes the whole fall, doesn't implicate anyone else. He admits to an uncontrollable urge to bash a gay guy, whatever. That's our deal with him."

"But you need Hubble, to get to Weston."

"Probably. But I'm after even bigger fish."

"Who?"

"Have you heard of James Forster?"

"Yes, I have."

"Well, he's my big fish."

Mock-admiringly, Esterbrook shook his head. "You've got a flair, Pete. No question."

"You want to hear how it goes?"

"Please."

"Hubble goes on trial, as advertised. He'll probably get an acquittal. That's because James Forster will have provided Hubble's defense with a high-priced, can't-miss lawyer. Forster also lays fifty thousand dollars on Hubble. When Forster does that, he's vulnerable, and we've got him by the balls."

"Oh. You've got James Forster by the balls. I see."

"He's already given us his game plan. All we have to do is turn it around on him. No problem."

"On what charge?"

"Obstruction of justice."

"Based on finding Hubble walking around with fifty thousand of Forster's money in his pocket. Is that the plan?"

As Esterbrook spoke, Hastings's pager sounded. He glanced at the digital display, grunted once, signaled for Esterbrook's scratch pad. Watching, Friedman saw the surprise in Hastings's face.

"Well?" Friedman said. "What?"

"It's Harold Best. He's in town."

Friedman blinked. "In San Francisco?"

Hastings nodded.

"And you're supposed to call him?"

Hastings shrugged. "What else?"

42

"My God," Ann breathed. "You scared me. You said you'd be back tomorrow, probably."

In the narrow entry hallway of Ann's ground-floor flat, Hastings maneuvered his suitcase, kissed her lightly before he closed the front door, tested the lock, and followed her into the living room, where he deposited his bag on the floor beside the bookcase. The TV screen displayed silent black-and-white images of a nightclub scene in an old movie that was familiar to him.

"*Casablanca*?" he asked. As, yes, Bogie appeared, clenching his jaw. How many thousands had that characteristic mannerism added to Bogart's income over the years? How many millions?

"Right. *Casablanca*." She picked up the TV wand, switched off the movie.

"No—that's all right. Leave it on."

"I know it by heart. Have you eaten? There's some chicken in the fridge. Scalloped potatoes, too."

"I'll take a look." He walked down the Victorian flat's long hallway, back to the kitchen. He found the chicken pieces, plastic-wrapped. He got a plate, scooped up a serving of potatoes, took a drumstick and a wing, and returned to the living room. As he ate, he recounted the interview with James Forster. Friedman had ordered him not to reveal that, perhaps at that very moment, Friedman and Best were meeting.

"Ah," she breathed, "you and Pete—it sounds like you're in over your heads."

"We just go where the investigation takes us. I'll tell you, though, life was a hell of a lot simpler without Harold Best and company. And a lot more predictable, too."

"Predictable . . . when is life ever predictable?" She smiled. It was a wan, wistful smile. Her mood had shifted. In the past many weeks—since Janet Collier had come into his life—he'd often seen Ann smiling like this as she searched his face for something she knew was no longer there.

She knew, and he knew. He could feel the guilt revealing itself on his face, naked to her gaze.

But what guilt? He'd once held hands with Janet Collier. He'd once told Janet—awkwardly confessed—that he was in love with her. He yearned to go to bed with her, become her lover. And she felt the same.

Yet except for a momentary adolescent groping in the police parking lot garage, they'd never touched each other. It was a Victorian dilemma begun, incredibly, in a serial killer's bedroom and played out in a nondescript Chinese restaurant around the corner from the Hall.

While behind his back the men and women of the Inspectors' Bureau sniggered. Because office romances were for losers. And Janet couldn't afford to be a loser. Not with a teenager to raise, not with a mother to help support.

"You're looking grim," Ann said.

"Am I?" He tried to smile—but failed. Now they were facing each other across the coffee table, he in an armchair. "I guess I'm not used to dealing with high rollers." He bit into a chicken thigh, contemplated returning to the kitchen for a bottle of seltzer water. He glanced at his wristwatch: eight thirty on a Saturday evening.

"Where're the boys?"

"Victor has them. They had a chance to go sailing this afternoon, and Victor had promised them a double feature. So they're staying at his place tonight. They'll come back tomorrow."

"Do I remember your saying that Victor has a new car?"

She nodded. "Another Porsche. Zero to sixty in some phenomenal time. That's one reason the boys are hanging around with him this weekend."

"What about Victor's girlfriend? Where's she go, when the boys sleep over?"

"I never asked." In the words, he could clearly hear the hard edge of anger. Never would she forgive Victor Haywood for leaving her in favor of another woman—or women. Haywood was a small, fastidious man who favored blue blazers, black tasseled loafers, and sometimes ascots.

Hastings finished the chicken thigh, ate a few potatoes, rose to his feet. "I'm going to get some Shasta water. Anything?"

"No, thanks."

When he returned to the living room and looked into Ann's face, he could clearly see her distress. It was a pain that had been aggravated by the mere mention of her ex-husband. Sitting to face her, he drank from the Shasta bottle and began again on the potatoes. Ann was an accomplished cook, and scalloped potatoes was one of her premier recipes.

He'd almost finished the potatoes when he heard her say, "I promised myself that the next time we were together, alone, without the boys in the house, I'd—" She broke off, blinked, momentarily lowered her head. But not before he glimpsed her stricken face. He put his fork on his plate, pushed the plate aside. And waited. She sat for another long moment with head bowed, hands clasped cruelly in her lap. Finally, with great effort, she raised her eyes to meet his. Her eyes were shining, wet with tears. When she finally spoke, it was to beg him for help: "You know what I'm trying to say."

He nodded. "Yes, I know what you're trying to say." He spoke slowly, gravely. For months, he'd known this moment was coming. Now he must help her, somehow ease her pain. But where were the words? If he could help her, who would help him?

"It's so—so goddam—" Helplessly shaking his head, he broke off. Then, desperate to say something, anything, he blurted out: "It's so complicated. So complicated and so—so sad."

"I—I hate to ask this." She spoke hesitantly, apologetically. "But I've got to know. Did the two of you ever—?"

Quickly, sharply, he shook his head, raised a hand in protest. "No. Never. We—I have to say—we talked about it. But, no, we've never made love. We've—it's strange to say it—but we've only really kissed once. Just once. And we—"

"She's a policewoman. Is that it?"

He nodded. "We worked a case together, months ago. It was

an accident, really. She was filling in. But that's how it started. She'd never seen a dead man, not in the line of duty. And so I—I tried to help."

Suddenly bitter, she laughed. "My God, that's a twist. I mean, usually it's the water cooler, in an office. Where was it, that you met? A back alley?"

"It was in a bedroom—the dead man's bedroom. We just held hands. Like—like two kids. Just like two kids."

For a long, silent moment, each avoiding the other's gaze, they sat silently. Then, with infinite reluctance, she said, "You have to move out. You've got to sleep on the couch tonight. And tomorrow, you've got to move out. Early. Before Victor brings the boys home."

"I know. I—that's what I want, too. But I don't want to lose track of the boys. Or you, either. I don't want to lose track of you."

Still looking away from each other, they sat in silence. Finally he said, "How long have you known?"

"About two months, I guess. It started as a feeling—a distancing. And when we—" She broke off, began again in a whisper: "When we made love, there was a difference. I—women feel these things, more than men. The sex, I mean. The difference in the sex, how it feels."

He watched her for a moment, waited for her to go on. But she said nothing. She was staring down at her clasped hands. Her cheeks were wet, and she cleared her throat painfully.

"Did you—do you want to know anything about her? Her name? Would you—?"

Once more, bitter laughter erupted.

"Oh, Frank. You're so—so innocent. So goddam innocent. That's what I'll miss. Your innocence."

He could think of no reply.